CARIBBEAN KIDNAP

In the Caribbean sunshine Fortune Island appears to be a peaceful spot – a fitting refuge for a wealthy man like Edward Dempster, but when James Hellier visits the island he finds it anything but peaceful. He is in search of a job, instead he finds dead bodies and a frightened woman who has mislaid her husband. He meets a crippled gunman who has hostile manners and later Senor Ramon – a softly spoken fanatic, with an uninhibited niece and a gang of deluded patriots.

CARIBBEAN KIDNAP

by

Michael Cronin

Dales Large Print Books
Long Preston, North Yorkshire,
BD23 4ND, England.

British Library Cataloguing in Publication Data.

Cronin, Michael
    Caribbean kidnap.

    A catalogue record of this book is
    available from the British Library

    ISBN   978-1-84262-897-3 pbk

First published in Great Britain in 1969 by
Robert Hale & Company

Copyright © Michael Cronin 1969

Cover illustration by arrangement with Arcangel Images

The moral right of the author has been asserted

Published in Large Print 2012 by arrangement with
Watson, Little Ltd.

Dales Large Print is an imprint of Library Magna Books Ltd.

Printed and bound in Great Britain by
T.J. (International) Ltd., Cornwall, PL28 8RW

Prologue

The Hotel Victoria was by no means the most exclusive in Mercanda, but the view from the terrace in the early morning was right out of this world, and James Hellier had not yet been in residence long enough to take it for granted.

There was that endless expanse of silver-blue sea, the white shining curve of the beach, the fishing boats bobbing home after their night's work, the elegant palms leaning on the cliffs where the sea birds floated, the lush greenery, and the wonderful clearness of the air.

Out there on the terrace the first cigarette of the day had a tang all of its own. It even improved the coffee.

He had his own table under the awning, and since he had arrived there two days before he had been on his own, strictly from choice – there were, he had soon noticed, one or two roving ladies who would not have been offended at the offer of his company, but he had other considerations in mind.

For one thing, he was too short of currency for comfortable dalliance. Mercanda was a pleasant island in the sun, but it could mean nothing more to him than a brief stopping place on the way elsewhere, and elsewhere had to be with Edward Dempster and his offer of congenial employment. Most important.

The only other resident with whom he had exchanged more than a polite good-morning was Huber, a middle-aged representative for a firm of textile manufacturers in the States. Huber knew Mercanda and most of the adjacent islands, he was a friendly type, and Hellier found him easy to get on with.

They had swapped drinks at the bar in the evenings, and there had even been some vague suggestion of a round of golf, sometime.

Hellier was on his third coffee and second cigarette when he saw Huber coming over to his corner of the terrace.

'Morning,' said Huber. 'Mind if I join you?'

'Glad of the company,' said Hellier, and meant it. 'Coffee?'

'Thanks.' Huber lit one of his thin cigars. 'Best part of the day. You been down to the harbour yet?'

'No – did I miss something?' said Hellier.

'The frigate's just come in, a genuine ex-U.S. Navy frigate with all the fittings, Mercanda's own Navy. They been talking

6

about it long enough. Now here it is. Big deal. A Navy.'

'A frigate?' said Hellier. 'What on earth for?'

'Prestige, maybe.'

'I don't get it,' said Hellier. 'What are they nervous about?'

'Seasonal jitters, friend,' Huber smiled. 'Haven't you noticed all the uniforms and guns?'

'I have,' said Hellier. 'In fact, I've had an encounter with them, two lads in nice clean uniforms, very smart and quite polite. I was walking down by the beach yesterday evening and they arrived out of nowhere and escorted me back to the road – after they'd checked everything I had on me. So what's the local crisis?'

Huber removed his cigar. 'Oil,' he said. 'There's a rig from the States been operating off the north cape, they expect to hit oil any day now – then you watch Mercanda boom … they don't want any outsiders horning in, stands to reason.'

'Then I'm glad I'm moving on tomorrow,' said Hellier.

'It's been quiet in Mercanda for a long time,' said Huber. 'A stable government, as honest as most in this area, so they don't want to take any chances… I've seen what's likely to happen when you bring in oil – it attracts the sharks quicker than a gold strike. They don't want any of that here. Very delicate situation developing.'

'I'll be happy to avoid it,' said Hellier. 'How about that round of golf before the sun gets too fierce?'

'I can accommodate you,' said Huber lazily. 'Ten dollars side bet suit you?'

'Robbery,' said Hellier. 'You're on.'

He won and left Mercanda early the next morning. The frigate, lean and grey, was in the harbour, with an admiring crowd on the quayside.

Chapter One

As they came round into the tiny bay there was nobody there to meet them, which was odd, Hellier thought. Middle afternoon with the sun just over the peak. Hot, but all right on the water. Enough of a breeze.

The island looked attractive, all those shades of green, just poking up out of the flat calm; easy to miss at night if you weren't too good in a boat; all that water all around.

Steff shifted about and squinted into the sun; a thin bony and very brown man with large bare feet and little hair; he looked like a waterfront tramp, but the boat was his and it was in good shape if you didn't take too much notice of paintwork and miscellaneous fish smells, especially when the engine warmed.

They slid towards the short wooden jetty; there was no other craft in sight.

'You sure he expecting you?' said Steff.

'He is,' said Hellier.

Where the jetty joined the white curve of the sand there were some wooden buildings, flat-roofed; oil drums stacked along the side in a tidy line; pieces of timber. Nobody came out to watch their quiet arrival.

Steff brought them in gently, reached up and held the boat steady against the wooden support. 'Have yourself a ball,' he said.

Hellier slung his case up and clambered after it. Steff had been handsomely paid before they started, which was Steff's practice.

'Thanks for the ride,' said Hellier.

'See you sometime.' Steff went into reverse, cleared the end of the jetty, then he was heading out across the bay. He lifted one hand in a salute without looking back. He hadn't said much all the way over.

James Hellier picked up his case; now the sun was fierce on his back, and the wooden planks sounded under his feet as he walked to the beach. He was watching the path that went up among the bushes; that was where the house must be. Edward Dempster would appear in a minute.

He was arriving right on the dot, which he thought pretty good and efficient: it was a hell of a small island, eighteen miles from anywhere. So now where was this prospective employer to take note of his punctuality and reliability? James Hellier thought of a long cool drink, chinking with ice, in the shade somewhere up beyond those bushes.

Before he had crossed the shining white sand he stopped and took off his jacket and rolled up his shirt sleeves. When he turned to look back Steff and his boat were well out.

Their arrival couldn't have been un-observed, not at a place as small as this; from the high ground the whole of the surrounding sea would be open to view. And where was Dempster's boat? Steff said he had a cruiser, twin-engined job, sea-going; perhaps the island had another bay with an anchorage.

He started up the narrow path – crushed white coral streaked with pale pink. He had signed nothing with Dempster, not yet. So perhaps he'd invite him to stuff his job, bonuses and all. He saw the house, on a flat elevation with trees behind it; a long bunga-low with white walls and a long sloping green roof that toned in with the trees; a veranda ran the length of the front; there were flowering bushes, white and purple and savage scarlet; plenty of white wood work and green awnings.

The bungalow didn't look all that big, but Dempster had said he didn't normally spend too much time on the island.

'My place of refuge from the world, Mr Hellier. One needs an oasis of quiet at times where none can intrude, don't you agree?' He had made the ownership of one's own private island sound like the most reason-able thing in the world. Money. You could think that way with enough money. That had been at their second meeting in Caracas. And from then onwards Hellier had found himself giving Dempster's proposition serious thought. Edward Dempster was an unusual man, and not at all just another man with money.

So here James Hellier was. Ready and almost willing. He put his case down on the path, wiped his face, and whistled, to announce himself to anyone who might care to take note. There was a patch of thin grass in front of the bungalow, bright chemical green as though each blade had been newly painted; the path ran round the side of the grass, forked, and one branch led up to the veranda, while the other disappeared at the back.

There was no sound, not even from the sea, barely a stir of air. He wondered if the hired help would be allowed to walk on the grass; all the windows had their green shutters down against the afternoon sun; siesta time, clearly.

He had almost reached the veranda, using the path, when a door opened, and a woman came out and gazed down at him, frowning. She wore a white dress, with a short skirt and no sleeves; she had very good legs, he noticed that much automatically; shortish blonde hair; a good and even suntan, no makeup that he could notice at that distance; about thirty three or so, he guessed. Apart from that bluntly unfriendly frown, she could be attractive.

He smiled and took off his hat. 'Good afternoon,' he said. 'I'm looking for Mr Dempster.'

She moved out from the doorway to see him more clearly; there was a jagged scratch down one tanned leg; she looked harassed, and her skirt was crumpled; he could see the faint shine of perspiration at the corners of her mouth.

'Who are you?' she said.

'James Hellier. I'm supposed to see Mr Dempster here this afternoon … isn't he about? He's expecting me.'

She sucked in her lips, considering him, not at all certain of his respectability, evidently.

He waved his hand to indicate the surrounding area of ocean, still smiling. 'I haven't just popped in from across the road. I have an appointment with Mr Dempster—'

'You'd better come in,' she said, and he could recall more cordial invitations. He followed her in and noted the smudge on the trim seat of her skirt, as well as the instinctive grace of her movement as she turned in the room to face him.

It was a wide room, with bright rugs and a polished floor and some lounging chairs; no flowers, no ornaments; nothing to indicate the feminine touch anywhere; it might well have been a hotel room; pleasant enough, but impermanent; no books, no magazines;

13

all very tidy.

'You say you've come here by appointment?' she said.

'Is this so hard to believe?' he said mildly. 'It's a little off the beaten track. I'd like to see Mr Dempster, if I may.'

'So would I. I'm Mrs Dempster.'

Edward Dempster hadn't mentioned a wife; there had been no reason why he should, it wasn't exactly the kind of detail that might concern a prospective employee. Mrs Dempster was at least fifteen years younger than her husband, Hellier surmised, and at the moment she wasn't being very pleased with her missing spouse. She had clear blue eyes and there was plenty of snap and sparkle in them.

'He must be around here somewhere,' said Hellier.

'If he is I haven't been able to find him,' she said. 'It's most annoying. I came here specially to see him, and he knew I was coming, and now there's not a sign of him.'

'You don't mean the house is completely empty?' said Hellier.

'Look for yourself.' She sank into a chair and stretched her legs wearily. 'I've even scrambled about among those damn bushes, I've shouted myself stupid.'

'But there must be some domestic staff, surely?'

'One man does everything for Edward

when he's here. Cooking, cleaning, the lot. A Filipino. Ahen Toong, and he isn't here either ... the house is spotless, as usual, so they haven't been away long.'

'You don't live here then,' said Hellier.

'No. Would you care for a drink, Mr Hellier?'

'Very welcome,' he said. 'Thank you.'

She gave him a thin smile as she got to her feet and her hands went to her hair. 'I feel a wreck. When I heard you coming up the path I was sure it was Edward. I've been positively simmering here alone for hours.'

'Very disconcerting,' he agreed. 'I expect your husband will turn up any minute now.'

'He'd better, I don't propose to spend the night here, I'm flying on to Jamaica in the morning. What will you drink? I make a pretty lousy Martini, but I'm safe with a Tom Collins.'

'Suits me,' he said. 'Anything you're having.'

'There's a nice amenable man.' Her high heels tick-tocked sharply across the polished floor, she pushed back the door into the next room; he heard the chink of bottles and glasses. She was humming softly to herself. He stood and looked out through the blind; the bungalow was pleasantly sheltered, but there was a wide expanse of sea spread out down there. He was wondering how Mrs Dempster had arrived, and how long

Edward Dempster would be; it was odd that he had pushed off just when he knew two visitors would be coming over the water to see him, and one of them his wife.

They didn't appear to be living together. Probably that was why Dempster hadn't mentioned her. He must be hard to please.

'Help yourself to cigarettes,' she called out. 'I won't be a moment.'

When she came back with the drinks she had tidied her hair, and her face looked fresher. She was, he decided, a very attractive woman. It was going to be no hardship to spend the time in her company while they waited for the return of her husband.

'Cheers,' she said, raising her glass. 'You're English, aren't you? My mother came from Sussex, I was at school over there for a while. I still like to go back whenever I can fit it in; do you know Sussex, Mr Hellier?'

'I used to do some sailing from Bosham, lost more than I could afford more than once at Goodwood … yes, I know Sussex. Your very good health,' he said.

'Excuse me.' She kicked off her shoes, bent over and massaged her toes. 'I didn't come exactly equipped for rambles … you must have urgent business with my husband, to come all this way.'

He smiled. 'I'm not fresh out of England, I've been in these parts for some time. As a matter of fact, I'm here at you husband's

16

invitation to discuss the offer of a job with him. It was his idea, coming here.'

She looked thoughtful. Then she said: 'Well, I hope it works out all right for you, he isn't the easiest of men most of the time. What are you, an accountant, Mr Hellier? Or another attorney? He's got flocks of them.'

'Just a willing hand,' he said. 'Personal assistant was the expression your husband used.'

She laughed shortly. 'That could be made to cover a lot of ground. I hope you'll enjoy it.'

'You are too kind.'

'I'm bitching. Sorry. It's no concern of mine, and you look capable of taking care of yourself. You may have gathered by now that my husband and I aren't compatible.'

'It happens,' he said in a carefully neutral voice.

'I mustn't prejudice you.'

He said nothing.

'Are you married, Mr Hellier?'

'I was. She's dead.'

'I'm sorry, that was clumsy of me.'

He took some of his drink. 'Don't bother yourself. It was some years ago.'

With the tip of one finger delicately she stroked the line of her throat, her eyes now half closed, looking away from him.

'No children?'

'None, fortunately.' Abruptly he finished

his drink and stood up. 'Have you any idea where your husband might be? Where I could look for him? His boat wasn't at the jetty down there.'

'I don't know,' she said. 'I've looked as far as I could, it's not very big but there's a hell of a heap of jungle covering most of it. I can't imagine where he might be, but with his boat gone that must mean he left the island, for some unknown reason. Damn the man, it's most inconsiderate of him.'

'Probably out fishing, with the Filipino.'

She shook her head. 'Edward loathes fishing, Toong always goes out on his own.'

'I'll take a look around,' said Hellier.

'You don't mind if I don't come with you. I've had my fill of the jungle out there, and the sun. Mr Hellier, suppose Edward doesn't turn up in time with his boat, will you take me back with you before it's dark? I do have to be on that plane in the morning.'

'We have a problem,' he said. 'I sent my boat back, Mrs Dempster. I was expecting to spend the night here, that was the arrangement with your husband.'

She sat up straight. 'Damn.'

'How did you get here?' he said.

'Hired a cruiser, early this morning. Edward or Toong would take me back, one of them always did.'

Those blue eyes had darkened with anger.

18

'What a stupid muddle!' Barefoot she strode across the room, her shoulders hunched, hugging her elbows, that tight skirt tugging at her thighs with every step. She stood and glared out through the slatted blinds.

James Hellier kept his peace. Edward Dempster was due to get an earful when he showed up.

'Typical, just typical,' she muttered savagely. 'No thought for anybody but himself! I might have known as much ... stuck here waiting for him!'

Hellier slipped out on to the veranda. The lady had a beef. Better to keep out of the way. Never get between a pair of embattled spouses – and Mrs Dempster did appear to have a legitimate grievance.

He had left his case on the veranda, he draped his jacket over it; but he kept his hat because the sun still had plenty of power. Now where to start looking? He knew it was only going to be a gesture; he would aim for the high ground and a clear slight of the sea so that he could spot Dempster's boat coming in, then he could nip down to the jetty and warn him of the impending tirade he could expect from his not so loving helpmate.

Mrs Dempster had been so right: there was a hell of a tangle of jungle once he got clear of the surrounds of the bungalow. At the back there was what looked like a small concrete block-house with tiny windows, with cables running in the rear of the premises; the door was unlocked and he looked in on a small power plant; then he recalled noting the electric lights in the front room.

There would probably be some kind of a pump for the water supply. Edward Dempster didn't believe in living rough on his island, that much was sure. There was a small tidy patch of vegetable garden, no doubt tended by the Filipino handyman, Ahen Toong.

'An oasis of quiet' Dempster had called it. Madame was due to ruin his tranquillity pretty damn soon. Hellier found a bit of a path that straggled through the bush, but after a hundred yards or so it died off, and he decided he'd need a hatchet to make any further progress. There had to be an easier route. His shirt was sticking to him, and his face streamed.

He wiped himself off with an already sodden handkerchief, lit a cigarette, and sat down to regroup his dwindling forces. This was surely no way to latch on to a new job, no matter what lucrative terms had been suggested. If Mister Edward Ruddy Dempster couldn't find it convenient to keep appointments he had made himself in this inaccessible spot he could find himself another lad. To hell with this feudal touch in a Caribbean jungle.

It was close and still, and he could hear the busy humming of insects in the nearby bush. Then he noticed the ants, the thick wavery stream of them crossing the path and pushing into the bush; great ginger hairy ants; all going one way and looking like a moving stream of treacle; he felt his skin crinkle and got to his feet in a hurry and brushed his trouser legs and stamped his feet.

He was about to move off when he caught sight of the piece of white cloth low down in the bush, and suddenly he was aware of the smell of putrefaction. Carefully he parted the leaves, and his stomach turned over so that he had to turn aside and wait for the nausea to pass, and he had to make himself look again.

The ants had found it, and some obscene furry animals the size of squirrels but with pink bellies and short coats – they rustled off among the undergrowth, but the ants continued with the mass excavation. It was the body of a man in a white singlet and pale blue cotton slacks; very little hair, a thick neck and short muscular arms, a hairless pale yellow skin.

The body lay on its front with the face turned outwards; dark dried blood covered one cheek down to the folds of the neck, and the ants had swarmed on what little was

21

left; the body still wore leather thonged sandals, and the white singlet had been pulled up clear of the back as though in a struggle, a losing struggle; there were broken branches to show where the body had been thrown.

Gagging violently, Hellier found his way down the path and into some clean air. That could be the body of Ahen Toong, it certainly wasn't that of Edward Dempster.

With the side of the face smashed in like that, and the body hidden in the bushes, that could only mean murder. So what about Dempster?

There were too many possibilities, and all of them were far from pleasant. He looked at the uninviting spread of vegetation all around; it would need an army with machetes to check it all properly. His stomach had stopped churning and his mouth tasted sweeter. He was trying to estimate just how long the body had been lying there; long enough for decomposition to set in – he could guess no more than that. It might have been there some days, hidden away from the sun. That made the matter of the missing Edward Dempster all the more important and pressing.

He started down the path towards the bungalow. This wasn't going to be enjoyable.

Chapter Two

She was out on the veranda, in a long lounging chair; he thought at first that she was sleeping, but when he reached the steps he saw that she was watching him; she didn't appear so angry any more, just tired of waiting.

'It really is too hot for that kind of thing, isn't it?' she said lazily. 'You look bushed.'

'It's hot enough,' he said.

'Come into the shade and relax,' she said. 'You look positively ill from your exertions.'

He took a seat beside her. 'Mrs Dempster, could you describe Ahen Toong for me?'

'Why?' Her voice was still lazy. 'He's a middle-aged Filipino, they mostly look alike, why do you ask?'

'About forty years old, not much more than five feet tall, not much hair on his head, wearing a white singlet and blue trousers – does that sound like him?'

Her eyes were wide open. Gripping the arms of her chair, she levered herself up. 'Then you've seen him? Where?'

'Under the bushes, up there, behind the house. He's dead, I'm afraid. Been murdered.'

She stood up. 'And Edward?'

He shook his head. 'Sorry, no sign of him.'

She started to move across the veranda. 'Take me there,' she said. 'Show me–'

'No,' he said. 'It wouldn't do any good, believe me.'

She was staring at him but he didn't think she really saw him all that clearly.

'Mrs Dempster,' he said gently.

'What about Edward? Didn't you see anything? Let me go up there–'

'No,' he repeated.

'You're sure?' she said, grasping at his arm.

'I saw no sign of your husband ... we mustn't jump to conclusions...'

'Murdered?' she said woodenly. 'But who? Who could have done it? Poor Toong, he never harmed anybody ... he was such a kind and gentle person, always smiling ... you could never be angry with him...'

She sat, her hands tight in her lap. 'I always hated this place, I couldn't bear it right from the first, and now look what happens...'

Her shoulders shook, but there were no tears, and he left her alone for a while; they still had the bigger problem right there ahead of them.

Presently she said: 'If you're thinking that Edward did it you're wrong, Mr Hellier.'

He had lit a cigarette. He glanced briefly at her. 'I don't have any theories, not at this stage.'

'You must have been thinking that,' she said.

'It crossed my mind. All we have is one dead body, and your husband is missing, so is his boat, I don't know what it adds up to.'

She had been holding her breath; now the words came out in a quick tumbling rush: 'You don't know either of them – it's unthinkable, Edward could never have hurt Ahen, never, I never even heard him raise his voice at him, not once ... and I've been married to Edward for twelve years, and Toong had been with my husband longer than that ... he was the soul of loyalty, why, he would rather have died than–'

She halted, there was no need to finish.

'Maybe that was why it happened,' said Hellier quietly.

'Listen to me,' she said. 'I want you to understand this. I know I wasn't a very satisfactory wife to Edward, it's years since we had anything in common ... and we've been going our separate ways. God knows Edward has plenty of faults, but lack of self-control isn't one of them, he doesn't act on impulse, there's ice inside him... I could never provoke him, and I tried hard enough in the early days – and I'm not talking about the bedroom either–'

'All right, all right,' said Hellier, 'I'm with you, so Toong met his death at the hands of somebody else. Tell me, does your husband

25

keep a gun here?'

'I don't think so,' she said. 'I wouldn't know about that, I never stayed very long here. Why do you ask? Was Ahen shot? Was that how he died?'

'All I saw were serious wounds to his face, and they weren't made by bullets, not as far as I could judge.'

She shuddered.

'I'd say a pretty savage assault before the body was thrown under the bushes. Perhaps last night, or sometime yesterday ... there was nobody around when you got here this morning, what time would that be, Mrs Dempster?'

'About ten or so,' she said. 'If I'd known then–'

'Damn good thing you didn't, that wouldn't have solved anything. Have you eaten since you got here?'

'Coffee,' she said. 'Some biscuits. I couldn't eat anything else, not now. What are we going to do?'

'We can still hope that your husband will turn up,' he said. 'We don't know that he won't.'

'You don't believe that,' she said shortly. 'And neither do I.'

'I'm optimistic by nature.'

'You asked about a gun,' she said, 'and that was because you think there may be somebody else here, somebody dangerous. I know, you don't have to wrap things up on my account, Mr Hellier.'

'I wouldn't think of it.' He was smiling, but she wasn't.

'We're both marooned here, for the time being,' she said. 'I realize that much.'

'Until your husband returns.'

'And in the meantime, what do we do? You must have some ideas.'

'We have about three and a half hours of daylight left,' he said. 'So I think I'll have another look around the territory.'

'Without a gun,' she said. 'Is that a good idea?'

'I should never have mentioned a gun,' he said. 'It was stupid.'

'No, you were being sensible ... stop treating me like a woman with the vapours – you'd feel happier if we had a gun, right? So let's search the place together. It shouldn't take long.'

It didn't take her long to conduct him through the bungalow. There were two large bedrooms, one of them Dempster's; there were no locked drawers in either of the bedrooms, and no other places where a gun might have been kept. In a corner of the living room there was a small desk and the top was locked; Hellier forced it open with a pair of pliers from the tool box in the kitchen; it held papers, business papers, and a photograph album with some snaps of Mrs

Dempster taken in the earlier and allegedly happier days of their marriage; the seaside snaps were particularly noteworthy: Mrs Dempster in a bathing outfit was featured prominently, and for excellent reasons.

Mrs Dempster's face was stony as she leafed through the album. 'I never knew he kept them,' she said, and put the pictures back. There was no gun. And by now Hellier knew they were wasting time.

Toong's room was at the back, near the kitchen; it was small, but as spotless as all the rest of the house; nothing locked. On the wall were some vivid pictures of the Madonna and Child; beside the tiny mirror there was a sad Christ on the Cross.

'Toong's one sorrow, when they came here,' said Mrs Dempster slowly. 'He couldn't get to Mass on Sunday … he was a good man. He deserved something better…'

Stooping, she fished under the end of the neat bed and brought up a pair of small white rubber soled shoes, very clean, almost new. Sitting on the edge of the bed she took off her shoes and tried on the white ones, then stood up.

'He wouldn't mind,' she said very softly. 'He always treated me like royalty. It shamed me.'

Carrying her own shoes she followed Hellier out into the kitchen. 'I'm coming with you,' she said. 'I could never manage in high heels.'

'I suppose I couldn't talk you out of it?' he said.

'You couldn't. Leave me here on my own? No thank you. Besides, I know a little about the place, you don't. Shall we start?'

Out in the sunshine she gave him a rough outline of the island; without high heels she looked small and much younger in some way, and she wore a wide-brimmed cream straw hat, borrowed from her husband's wardrobe. All the higher ground was in the middle and northern part of the island, and she said they'd never hack their way through the middle; the stream they took their water from rose high up and flowed down past the rear of the bungalow, then cascaded down into a small bay with steep cliffs.

'It's kind of wedge-shaped,' she said, 'and we're on the pointed end down here, it's less than a mile long, but you can't hope to move in a straight line anywhere – and it's easy to get lost in all that jungle, I hate the sight of it ... we'd better keep close to the sea.'

In places the grass was waist-high, coarse and prickly, and the footing highly insecure; they had to paddle through the stream before moving along the coast, and it was fatal to lose sight of the sun in among the thick creepers and curtains of Spanish Moss. She was keeping up with him very well, and she didn't make any feminine complaints about the damage to her face or clothes. She was a lot tougher than she seemed, he reflected.

Deliberately he had kept her away from the area where he had found Ahen Toong's body, and she hadn't asked him about it. He was looking for signs of another body and pretending to himself that he wasn't. In all that tangled jungle a body could lie undetected for ever.

She was allowing him to offer her a helping hand now and then over the rougher spots, but when he suggested a halt and perhaps a return she shook her head.

'I'll finish it on my own,' she said. 'If you don't want to come ... we're looking for my husband, aren't we?'

He could do no more than nod and wipe a dirty face on an equally dirty forearm. 'You're just about flaked out,' he said.

'I'm all right,' she insisted. 'I know what we came for ... and we haven't nearly finished.'

'We've covered a couple of hundred yards in about half an hour,' he said, 'but we'll continue if you say so.'

He grinned at her with more cheerfulness than he knew might be justifiable. 'So long as we make sure we can get back before it's dark ... we'll probably find your husband waiting for us back there at the house.'

'That would be nice,' she said thinly. 'I'll be keeping it in mind.'

Her face was streaked with sweat and dirt, her damp hair was tangled about her forehead, and the late Ahen Toong's shoes were no longer white. She had a tear in her skirt from mid-thigh to hem, and there was nothing she could do about it.

They went on, not talking so much now, there were other uses for the little breath they had left; they had come through a marshy patch where their feet had squelched most unpleasantly, well over their ankles in warm black slime, filthy black bubbles bursting as they moved on, and a stench of rotting vegetation. It was the worst so far.

'If there's much more of this we'll have to turn back,' he said, and this time she gave him no argument, she was much too occupied with trying to keep her footing and not think about the unmentionable things they might be disturbing in the muck, and she had to hold on to his arm. The smell was unbeatable, and by the time they fought clear to the dry ground he was all-but carrying her.

She was on the point of collapsing as he helped her up to where the mangroves crowded to the edge of the swamp. He found some dry roots and made her sit with her back against his knees.

'That wasn't very fragrant,' he said.

Her shoulders shook spasmodically. 'I want to be sick—'

He bent and held her head and made the acceptable soothing sounds, and she said she felt better afterwards. He got her to her feet slapping viciously at the mosquitoes.

'We'd better keep moving,' he said.

'Just don't look at me,' she murmured. 'I don't think I'll ever feel really clean again.'

Then he knew she was better. They were on firmer ground. To their left was the green mass of the higher land, sloping down, so he could guess that they had somehow managed to traverse most of the length of the island. They'd have to dodge that blasted swamp on the way back.

'Hey,' he said, 'I think I can see the sea again, look, we must be nearly at the top end.'

She peered with him through the leaves. 'Yes,' she said. 'Ahen Toong used to go fishing there, by the reefs.'

A little further on he was able to lead her out into the open and the sunshine, where the air was suddenly sweet. The sea was a deepening blue spread out before them.

'Cigarette?' he said.

She shook her head. 'There's a boat down there,' she said. 'I think it's Edward's – don't you see? On the outer reef...'

Chapter Three

He forgot his cigarettes and moved beside her to see what she was looking at so intently.

'Don't you see?' she said. 'Out there?'

The flat bright surface of the sea was broken here and there by the scattered tips of coral, where the slow tide made a faint tracery that would be boiling white foam if the wind rose. The sun picked out the gleaming paintwork of a boat that seemed to be squatting sideways on one of the furthest reefs, with the bows tilted higher than the stern – by no means a happy sight.

'That's Edward's boat all right,' she said, a little bitterly. 'He should never have run it in so close, he knows it's dangerous, Ahen always warned him ... that reef must have torn her bottom to shreds – he was never much good at handling a boat.'

'Can he swim? It's not too far out.'

'Too far for him,' she said. 'He'll be still on board.'

'Yes,' said Hellier, but something told him that she was talking mostly to convince herself. 'It must have been high tide when he ran her on the reef,' he said, 'otherwise the chances are that he'd have floated off if he'd done it at low water – I wonder if the tide's high now?'

'The reefs always look pretty much like that,' she said. 'Except when it comes on to blow, then it all looks worse. The tides don't rise much usually – he must have been crazy to think he could take her through there...'

Crazy or desperate, Hellier thought. She was taking it for granted that her husband had been on board. It was a reasonable assumption, perhaps. Hellier's sight was excellent, but he could detect no sign of any movement on the wreck, and he knew she was looking for the same thing.

It was, he reckoned, about four hundred yards out. Not a difficult swim, if you were a fair swimmer, and he was rather better than that. They were going to do no good, standing there and looking ... and speculating. And from the expression on her stained face he knew he would have to do something.

He searched for a way down to the water's edge. There was no beach there, just rocks, all the way down. Not too far and not too steep.

'You stay here,' he said. 'I'll bring him back.'

She said something as he began to clamber down the rocks, but he was too busy to listen, and he didn't look back at her. It was tricky and he had to be careful. If he slipped and broke a rib they'd both be in real trouble. To his already pungent body odour he added a liberal coating of seaweed and rank slime of a brilliant green. He thought very briefly about sharks and barracuda. That wasn't a sheltered lagoon out there, he'd be swimming out into the open sea; it was not a comforting thought.

He reached an outcrop of rock that appeared to shelve into the sea. It was too late to have second thoughts, not with her standing up there and watching his heroic endeavours. He stripped down to his underpants and lowered himself into the water; it was a private relief to begin feeling clean again; the sea was fine and refreshing; he struck out for the outer reef, using a long-distance crawl, and checking his line every twenty yards, but so far there didn't seem to be any strong current pulling him off his route.

He made himself think of nothing but the rhythm of swimming, and most of the time the water was so clear that he could see the sandy bottom and the small bright darting fish. When he estimated that he was two thirds of the way there he turned on his way back for a breather, and lifted one arm to give her a wave.

She had climbed down to where he had entered the water, and she seemed to be as near naked as would make no difference. Very picturesque against the dark rocks in the sunshine. About to give herself a refreshing dip while she waited.

He didn't wave, he turned over and resumed his progress. The clear sandy bottom had gone when he got into the area of the reefs, and he had to be doubly careful because he didn't want to lose an acre or so of skin on the coral; the sea was cloudy and greener now, not so warm, with little wavelets slapping his face.

He was near enough to read the name stencilled in gold and black across the boat's stern: *Torquil Two*. He trod water and shouted, but nobody looked over at him. So he swam in and held on to the rudder. She must have hit the reef at a fair old clip, to judge from the way her bows were wedged, and he could feel jagged edges of coral under his feet when he let them trail down in the water.

'Anybody aboard?' he shouted. Only the rudder creaked as he worked himself around to get aboard; an obviously expensive sea-going cruiser, with accommodation amidships and good lines. Teak decking and paintwork that still dazzled.

He flopped over the side and into a spacious well-deck, and found it inches deep in sea, and now he was sure he wasn't going to find anybody aboard. She had been driven hard on the reef and then aban-doned. Nobody in his right senses would have jammed a boat there except by accident.

Automatically his hand went to the twin casings of the engines, and they were no warmer than he might have expected from the sun; there was none of the oily smell of machinery recently in use. As he moved he could hear the harsh relentless grinding of the coral against the timbers. She lay just a few degrees off an even keel, and water slopped about gently wherever he looked; if she ever got off the reef she would sink like an old tin kettle.

There'd be cabin accommodation for five or six. He looked into the galley, all neat and shipshape: Sink, stove, racked utensils just where they should be, secured cupboards properly shut; no food had been prepared there for some time, he guessed; there was a St Christopher medallion tacked to a bulkhead.

He could see through into the saloon, where the light was filtered a soft green-blue through the glass panels. There were padded bunks along the sides, a table on a central pedestal. He slid the door along and it stuck.

Then he saw the legs of the body of a man, lying face-down under the table, one arm curled around the pedestal, the small white-handled automatic, almost within reach of the curled fingers. Carefully he stepped over the sprawling legs, stooped and turned the body over just enough to see its face.

Edward Dempster wasn't going to have any further need for a personal assistant; he had been shot low down in the stomach, apparently, and there was an ugly dark-rimmed hole just below the neck, as though the bullet had gone through the middle of his body, upwards; the blood had long since dried, and this time there were no ants. But Dempster's upper dentures had slipped into a macabre grin, and Hellier was happy to lower the body and step clear.

There was no evidence of any struggle, yet it couldn't have been suicide, not if one bullet had been fired so as to travel upwards through the thickest part of the body. He picked up the small automatic, handling it carefully between finger and thumb and only by the short barrel; it had a full clip, and the bullets were too small to make those dark holes. Suppose Dempster had been bending backwards, perhaps over the edge of the table, when he was shot? The murderer could have rammed his gun forwards and then fired...

He looked around the saloon. Just above the bunk on the other side there was a splintered hole in the panel, and it was at the right height, he thought. There was no mark on the dark polished surface of the table.

Faint slapping and panting sounds came from the stern, and he heard her calling urgently: 'Mr Hellier ... Mr Hellier – help me...'

He closed the door of the saloon, swore quietly to himself, and went quickly aft through the saloon. He saw her head and shoulders, and her groping arms; she had been trying to pull herself aboard and the effort twisted her face. 'Please,' she gasped, 'I can't do it by myself...'

He gave her a heave up. She wore white briefs, transparent with the wet; nothing more. She sat with her hands dangling between her knees, catching her breath, damp strands of hair swinging.

He had never found an attractive woman without her clothes less welcome. Presently she thrust the sodden hair clear of her face and looked up at him.

'Did you find anything?'

'Yes,' he said. 'It's not good, I'm afraid.'

'Tell me ... is it Edward?'

He nodded.

'You've found him? Where?' She stood, a slim pale brown figure, shoulders and the tips of her breasts shining from the sea. 'Where is he?'

He tried to hold her, but she slipped past him and went into the galley. He remained where he was for long minutes before following her, and even then he halted at the door of the saloon. She was kneeling beside the body and all he could see was the long gentle curve of her back. She didn't need him and he wouldn't know what words might fit.

So he shifted aft and gave himself another long look at all the surrounding sea. Now two dead bodies to cope with. And the sorrowing widow.

Fortune Isle, that was what the late Edward Dempster had said was the name of the island. Not very good fortune for him or the faithful Ahen Toong. Somebody had a reason for all this, a motive. Somebody.

He gazed across at the rising green mass of the island. Shadows began to reach out across the water. In little over an hour the sun would be down. And then what?

When she came into the galley she wore a man's white cotton singlet; it came down below her waist and was loose on her except where her breasts pushed at the thin cloth, and there was a blankness in her face that was more eloquent than any paroxysm of noisy grief. She sat on the tall fixed stool by the sink. She had been weeping, but that was done with now.

'We can't just leave him there,' she said. 'Can we? It – it doesn't seem right ... just to go away and leave him.'

40

'We haven't a dinghy,' said Hellier. 'It would be a long way to tow – I might be able to do it.' He wasn't relishing the prospect, towing a dead body all that way, and Mrs Dempster didn't look as though she was fit to manage the return trip unaided.

'Isn't there a raft or a lifebuoy on board?' he said. 'Something we could use?'

'There's an inflatable rubber thing strapped to the top of the cabin,' she said. 'In the front.'

He went for'ard, found the unbuckled straps. Nothing else. Nothing at all that he could use. He went back and told her. She sat and covered her face with both hands, no sound from her.

He cleared his throat. Edward Dempster had been a biggish man, almost sixteen stone ... keeping the body afloat all the way, and coping with her...

'Let's get you back to the beach first of all,' he said quietly. 'Do you think you can make it?'

She moved her hands away. 'I'm only adding to your difficulties,' she said, 'coming here... I don't help much.'

'Not to worry,' he said. 'We'll arrange something, somebody will turn up to get us, soon – I promise you.'

She shuddered and gave him the ghost of a smile. 'He didn't kill himself, Mr Hellier, even I know that.'

41

He didn't say anything.

'Ahen Toong, now Edward ... who can have been doing these dreadful things here? Why? Why? What does it mean?'

'I wish I knew,' he told her soberly. 'We ought to be starting.'

'I suppose so,' she said and he had never heard such utter weariness in a woman's voice, such a profound lack of any wish to go on, to do anything that needed any conscious effort. 'It seems so wrong to leave him...'

'I know,' he said. 'We'll do something, later. We can't stay here.'

She slid off the stool and almost fell. He had an arm around her shoulders, feeling her shake against him as he coaxed her along aft to the stern. There seemed to be more water slopping about inside now, and he fancied the stern sat lower; the rocky beach appeared a long way off.

'I'll be with you all the way,' he said. 'Just take your time. All right? Nice and easy.'

She smiled again, a little stronger this time. 'You'll never know what a comfort you are.'

He dropped over the side and she followed him; she did a steady unhurried breast-stroke at first and he thought she'd make it without too much bother. He was keeping beside her so that she could see him all the time, and whenever he caught her eye he grinned encouragingly. She was doing a lot better than he had expected. She even varied the breast-stroke with quite a creditable crawl, but she couldn't keep it up, and she had to rest afterwards while he floated along with her and her hair spread darkly over her face.

She said she felt all right, and he told her they were almost there which was far from the truth and she knew it. Later on her stroke began to falter and she was missing her breathing, snatching at it and taking in some sea, her face contorted and her eyes desperate.

So he moved in front and under her, turned her on her back, gentling her and towing her slowly so that she could feel the support of his hands under her arms. He didn't hurry any of his movements although he was shipping some sea himself. She didn't panic, she allowed herself to be taken in charge, doing just what he told her, until she said she was able to go on.

The last stretch took them a long weary time, and her eyes were closed most of the way. A little touch of an offshore wind or current would have beaten them, but the sea remained calm and friendly. Slowly the beach came nearer.

He had to admire her determination, after what she had just been through on the boat back there. She kept going, her breathing hard and noisy. He had to tow her the last few yards. As soon as she could crawl on to a rock she flopped on to her stomach and panted.

He squatted beside her. 'Well done,' he said. 'Very well done.'

She rolled slowly over, sat up wearily. 'I'm going to be sick, I think.' And she was.

Chapter Four

Their clothes lay spread out flat on a rock. 'I rinsed them in the sea,' she said. 'I thought they might smell better.'

'Very noble of you,' he said. He put on his shirt, and it felt like thin warm cardboard. He was reaching for his trousers when he noticed the splash of bright orange further along among the rocks. She was wrestling with her dress, and her back was turned modestly, since she had taken off the white cotton singlet.

He paddled along beside the edge of the water, and he had already guessed what he was going to find. It was the inflatable rubber dinghy, wedged in among the rocks and partly covered by seaweed; it was designed to hold three or four persons, and from the way it was wrinkled he knew it had been punctured.

When he managed to free it from the rocks he saw the slit along the side, and the folds of rubber flopped about just under the surface. There should have been some paddles, but he saw none nearby.

Mrs Dempster had now joined him. 'We're not having much luck, are we?' she said bitterly. 'We could have used that.'

'I'm wondering how it got here,' said Hellier. 'It was strapped to the top of the cabin, it couldn't have broken loose, it's not possible. Somebody used it.'

He was sorry he had spoken when he saw the look on her face; her eyes strayed to the dark mass of land above them. She stood knee-deep in the water, the hem of her skirt lifted clear.

'It must have been Ahen Toong,' he said.

'Somebody else,' she said. 'He would never have left my husband on the boat alone.'

'There was a fight,' said Hellier, 'an argument–'

'And Toong shot my husband and ran off?' She shook her head. 'If you'd ever known Toong you couldn't think that.'

'All right,' he said. 'But I don't think the dinghy drifted here all on its own ... we'd better be starting back.'

Following him through the shallow water, she said: 'You mean there must have been other people here when it happened?'

'Unless your husband and Ahen Toong killed each other, which is not possible.'

'So then?'

He waited for her to catch up with him and he took her hand. 'There's no point in this, trying to guess ... we don't know enough – our immediate objective is to find a way back to the bungalow without having to go through all that swamp again, and we don't have all that much time before it's going to be dark. I hope you can cook because I'm getting hungry.'

They retrieved the rest of their clothes; her rubber soled shoes were all right; she had rinsed his socks, but they felt highly unpleasant inside his still sodden shoes; he put on his trousers and they climbed back to the top. Neither of them looked back out over the water to the boat on the reef.

She said one thing that indicated the way her mind was running: 'You didn't bring my husband's gun, did you? I saw it on the floor of the cabin.'

'We won't be needing it,' he said. 'I had nothing to carry it in, the sea wouldn't have kept it in good condition anyway … let's see if we can find a decent route down the west coast, it's no real distance, we shouldn't have to battle our way through all that jungle … how do you feel?'

'So so, I'll be all right, I can go where you can go.'

'I'm sure you can,' he said cheerfully.

'What do you really think happened about the rubber dinghy, Mr Hellier?'

'I don't know, I honestly don't know. My name is James, by the way.'

'Eileen,' she said.

Keeping close to the edge of the cliffs they were able to make reasonable progress for most of the way, following the sharp bends of the coast. Where the jungle ran down to the verge they had to clamber down and wade across, and once they had to swim and paddle through over a hundred yards of reedy rock-strewn water where long tendrils of weed twined themselves around their legs, and Eileen Dempster's lips were moving as though in silent prayer.

But she didn't hesitate to follow wherever he led, and he didn't have to spend any precious time waiting for her. A wonderful sunset was building up there out over the sea, but neither of them had any eyes for it.

They were a very bedraggled pair by the time they had heaved themselves up to the last headland and saw the small placid bay and the jetty down below them, and the roof of the bungalow among the trees. Then he relaxed and let her sit for a little while until she said she was ready to finish it.

When they reached the veranda she dropped exhaustedly into a chair and closed her eyes. He went through to the sitting room and then to the dining room beyond where she had gone for the drinks. There was a handsome cabinet and it held about every drink he had ever heard of and some he had never met. He was remembering how fussy Dempster had been about the wine when they had dined in Caracas.

He found cognac and glasses and poured

two man-sized drinks, and went back. She hadn't moved.

'Here,' he said, 'we both need it.'

She took the drink, swallowed it almost all, shuddered, drank again and got slowly to her feet. He thought she was going to collapse, but she didn't. Whatever else she might lack it wasn't courage.

Delicately she picked the sodden folds of her skirt away from her legs and wrinkled her nose at herself. 'I can cook,' she said, 'but I'll take the first shower if that's all right with you?'

He smiled and nodded, and she went in. He stood brooding over the cognac and looking out over the darkening scene. Somebody had come ashore back there in the rubber dinghy – somebody who knew about the deaths of Dempster and the loyal Ahen Toong? Somebody who had then left the island? He was wishing he'd had the presence of mind to do something about that gun in the cabin. A really intrepid type would have found some way – wrapped it in something and tied it on top of his head while he swam, something like that, something resourceful. But in his anxiety to get Mrs Eileen Dempster off that blasted boat he hadn't given the gun another thought, not until she had mentioned it.

It had been a hell of a shock for her, finding her husband like that. He could hear the hissing of the shower, and he was trying to recall just what she had said about her husband, but he could remember nothing beyond the fact that they evidently hadn't been living together.

He went inside and tried the lights and he was relieved to find they worked. He had a few cigarettes left in his case, and as he dragged the smoke down into his chest he realized how hungry he was – he was also aware of the strong fishy smell that clung to him, and the squelching of his toes inside his soaked socks. In his case he had a spare shirt, pyjamas, shaving kit, and some socks. According to Edward Dempster they would be spending only one night on the island. One night? He wasn't now ready to bet on it.

When she appeared she looked like a new and younger woman. She wore a sleeveless cream jersey, and a pale blue skirt; her hair was still damp, but curling at the ends, and her face clear and fresh, except for her eyes.

'Food in half an hour,' she said. 'I'll see what's available.'

'Fine,' he said.

'Did you bring any other clothes?' she said.

'A shirt, I travel light.'

'I'll arrange it.' She went into the kitchen, and he took his case into the bathroom. The late Edward Dempster didn't believe in missing any of the amenities on his island, the bathroom had all the gadgets, an over-size bath-tub and a shower stall; there was a chest developer fixed to one wall and a weighing machine.

He gave himself a leisurely shave and then stood under the shower; it proved so invigorating that he was tempted to burst into song, but resisted the temptation – the newly-made widow mightn't care for it. He ran the shower from cold to hot and back again, and he used up an amount of good quality soap.

He thought he heard the door open, but when he emerged with a large towel around his middle all he saw was the tidy bundle of clean clothes on the stool beside the door. There were dark blue cotton slacks, with the laundry creases still on them – Edward Dempster had been generously built about the middle, but a leather belt took care of the surplus; the thin leather slippers were a shade large, but he couldn't afford to be fussy, and his own shoes would dry.

She gave him a quick and comprehensive look when he arrived in the kitchen; there was a comforting smell of food on the way.

'Mostly canned stuff I'm afraid,' she said. 'But there's a salad … you can set the table if you like.' The electric fan on a shelf above the sink lifted her hair from her flushed face and made her appear softer and more vulnerable. Now it was dark outside, and there was a soft hushing sound of wind in the trees; it should have been a soothing sound, instead it was a reminder of their solitary condition.

He set the table and she brought in the soup – tinned asparagus; with the salad there was cold roast chicken, and he found himself eating most of it. She said very little, and that little grew less and less as the strange meal progressed.

When they got to the coffee he said gently: 'We'll have to talk, you know, make some plans.'

'I'm sorry,' she said. 'I'm being very rude.'

'I didn't mean that,' he said quickly. 'It's a rotten business—'

'Please,' she said.

'You don't have to apologize to me,' he insisted.

She smiled. 'Thank you, but now I have to tell you something, the real reason why I came here, the only reason – it makes it all the worse. I was going to ask him for a divorce. Can you imagine how that makes me feel now?'

He waited for a moment. Then said: 'Did he know?'

'He knew. We had discussed it before. He knew my feelings ... nice, isn't it? I feel such a bitch.'

'No,' he said.

She let him give her a cigarette, and her mouth was suddenly ugly. 'I despise myself.'

'You needn't,' he said. 'You won't, when you think about it later on.'

'How can you be so sure? It's not your problem.'

It was going to be very much his problem, he was thinking. Until they got off that island. Nothing was going to convince her that what had happened to her husband hadn't somehow been connected with her.

'How soon are people going to miss you?' he asked. 'People outside?'

She wanted a divorce, so there would be another man in the offing, and if he didn't want to know where she was he wasn't the kind of man she should be thinking of marrying. But Hellier didn't think he ought to spell it out for her.

'You said something about flying on to Jamaica in the morning,' he said. 'Meeting friends there?'

'Nobody who will worry too much if I don't show up for a day or so. I have a small rented place near Casa Blanca, there's a housekeeper who'll be expecting me, but she won't think anything about it if I don't arrive, she's used to me by now. I have friends there of course.'

'Of course,' he said.

She looked at him. 'Do I have to guess at what you're thinking? You're wrong, you know – I'm not planning to rush into another marriage.'

'So nobody is going to miss either of us right away,' he said. 'That might complicate things for us. Who else knew you were coming here?'

'I didn't shout it abroad.'

'You didn't mention it to anybody?'

'I saw no reason to. What about you, James?'

'There'll be no hue and cry for me. I came here to get myself a job. I didn't brag about it until it was sure, and it wasn't. I have a few acquaintances dotted about, but I've been moving around too much to make any real friends, people who might want to know where the hell I am. I gather there is no phone?'

'No,' she said. 'That was the whole point of having this place – nobody could get at him. He seldom stayed here very long, just the odd visit, a week here and there … the two of them. He didn't usually invite guests. This was his own private retreat, and he was quite jealous about it… I could never stand being here, I like people around me, and Edward and I didn't find much to say to each other, so there just wasn't much point in inflicting myself on him here. We didn't quarrel, don't think that, it was just that we had drifted so far, and I know I got on his nerves.'

She sounded bitter, dispirited. 'We couldn't have isolated ourselves more effectively – and I can't believe that Edward is dead, it doesn't seem real... I've never seen anybody dead before ... and like that. Like, like a dummy ... he didn't kill himself, did he? He couldn't have...'

Hellier shook his head. She was rubbing the stub of her cigarette into the ashtray, round and round, not looking.

'I can't get it out of my mind.' Her voice was nothing more than a whisper.

And he was glad that she hadn't stumbled across what had been left of Ahen Toong. Her eyes were beseeching him for some comfort.

'How long do you think it will be before somebody comes for us? It will be soon, won't it?'

'Well now,' he said. 'Your husband's plan was to leave here tomorrow, I know that much because he told me when I arranged to come. We'd be going across to Antigua, he said. He has an office there, hasn't he? When he fails to arrive they'll start making some kind of a check, and that will lead them here, it's the logical place to start.'

'Then it could well be days before anything happens?'

'I think not,' he said. 'A man like your husband can't just drop out of everything and not be missed, and from what he told me we'd be catching a charter flight at mid-day tomorrow at St Lucia, a British West Indies Airline, so that'll cause inquiries when we aren't there on time. Somebody will arrive here sooner than you think.'

'If you hadn't come,' she said, 'if I'd been here on my own, I wonder what I would have done?'

'You would have settled down here to the best of your ability, to wait, which is what we are going to do.'

Slowly she shut one hand into a fist. 'I'm frightened,' she said. 'I can't pretend I'm not.'

'I'd think you were a strange woman if you weren't.'

'They were murdered, weren't they? Both of them?'

He nodded.

She closed her eyes, her hands now folded together in front of her mouth, just touching her lips.

'So what can we do?' she whispered.

'Wait. And get some rest.'

'I won't be able to sleep ... it's unthinkable.'

'All right,' he said. 'We'll sit up all night if you like and talk and drink coffee. Tomorrow will come.'

'Talk,' she said, her eyes still closed. 'I'll listen, just go on talking to me, please ... tell me about yourself.'

'My very favourite topic,' he said. 'That'll take more than one night... I'm a gifted liar and I have a captive audience.'

She had opened her eyes and there was just the suspicion of a smile beginning around her mouth. 'Tell me how you first met Edward. How did he come to offer you a job?'

Chapter Five

'My native charm and good luck,' he said.

'My husband would have needed something more substantial than that,' she said, and the smile had broken out into the open.

'It was about a month ago, in Caracas. For a number of reasons, which aren't at the moment pertinent to this narrative, I found myself temporarily at a loose end, and I was not exactly enjoying the experience, if you take my meaning.'

'You were broke?' she suggested.

'Nearly flat,' he said, 'but in a gentlemanly sort of fashion, and Caracas is not the right place for a European to be short of currency – the slide downwards can be very quick and not at all good for the morale. So there was this prosperous gentleman who was having trouble with a large car. Ignition, but it had him baffled.'

'That sounds like Edward,' she said. 'Anything mechanical defeated him. So you fixed his car?'

'I did. It was nothing much, but it made him happy. He suggested a drink, and that is a suggestion I seldom refuse, especially in these latitudes. He seemed very friendly, I thought. One thing led to another, and when he invited me to dine with him that night I wasn't insulted – he had a nice tough attitude, and my hand wasn't out. Frankly, I found him very interesting.'

'He could be,' she said. 'All the money he had he made himself. Not many people could ever put anything over on him.'

'He was successful,' said Hellier. 'He must have made some enemies.'

'I wouldn't know about that,' she said briefly. 'He kept his business life to himself.'

Epitaph of a marriage.

Defensively she looked across at Hellier. 'I was never allowed to take any interest, even now I don't know all the affairs he was concerned with. I know he ran some export agencies, and he was developing some real estate interests, but I don't know any details. I honestly have no idea how rich he was. He was always generous, and I have a little money of my own.'

Lucky Eileen Dempster, with a marriage that had gone sour. Now she was a widow, and all she had wanted was a divorce.

'One thing I'd like you to understand,' said Hellier. 'I didn't ask your husband for anything. I wasn't that broke, I was just on a thin patch. It's happened to me before, and it'll probably happen again. A few days after we had first met your husband rang me at the dump where I had a bed and we met again. He must have guessed by then how things were with me, and he came out with the offer of a job. Three months probation in the first instance, and a reasonable salary. I would have to do some of his travelling for him, he said, checking on his agents here and there. It suited me fine, I had nothing to lose.'

'No ties?' she said softly.

'None that matter. I hope I have enough intelligence to get by without too much strain, and I know I'm honest.'

'Now you're out of a job,' she said.

He stood up and began to gather together the dishes. 'You relax,' he said. 'I'll see to this.'

'You don't live in a vacuum,' she said rising. 'You haven't told me anything real about yourself.'

He found a tray and stacked the plates. 'What would you like to know? We have all night. You mean women?'

'Well that would be a start,' she said.

'I like them, some of them.' He loaded the tray and took it out into the kitchen. Sooner or later, in his experience, most women seemed to get on to the same theme. They just had to know. He started on the washing up and he knew she was standing there in the open doorway watching him, so he made a great and busy clatter in the sink. Very domestic.

'You're a strange man,' she said. 'I wonder how you would have got on with Edward.'

'We'll never know.'

She moved over and took up a tea towel and began to dry some of the plates. Frowning. Almost husband and wife.

'We might be here some days,' she said.

'We might.'

'You don't seem very disturbed.'

'I'm disturbed all right,' he said. 'It's just that it doesn't show. British phlegm. You know.'

'What sort of things have you been doing? You don't mind me asking?'

'Not a bit of it.' It might help to keep her mind off her own immediate problems. 'Have you ever heard of a place called Isidro?'

'Vaguely. I've never been there.'

'Keep it like that,' he said. 'I had a job there of sorts. It blew up and I had to leave in a hurry. Nothing to my detriment, believe me. There was a girl in it.'

She smiled. 'Naturally. What happened?'

'Nothing of any lasting importance.'

'I doubt that,' she said. 'I can see it in your face.'

He put the last of the cutlery on the draining board, and rolled down his sleeves. 'She was a nice girl,' he said. 'Plenty of spirit, and in an awkward situation when I happened along.'

'Rather like me,' she said lightly.

'Up to a point, but I wouldn't press the parallel. We were both fugitives, the details don't matter. If the circumstances had been different something might have come of it. Perhaps.'

'And now you regret it? Be honest, you do, don't you? Were you in love with her?'

'What's the point? It's over now.'

'And you don't mind? That does sound so sad.'

In a moment she'd be feeling sorry for him. So he grinned at her. 'I wish we had a radio here, a little light music might help. Well now, that's the domestic chore out of the way. I suppose we're all right for food and so on?'

She nodded and he followed her into the living room. 'It's going to be a long night,' she said, a little wearily.

'It'll pass.'

'And then what do we do tomorrow?'

'Wait,' he said. 'Somebody will come here for us.'

'What was her name? That girl?'

'Susan,' he said. 'Susan Lugard.'

'Nice.'

'She was. More than that.'

'And you haven't forgotten her?'

'It wasn't all that long ago,' he said. 'A brief encounter.'

'I'm prying,' she said. 'Do you mind? Tell me about your Susan.'

'Well,' he said, 'if it will help to pass the time–'

They both heard it, the faint sound from outside on the veranda, a bump, then the soft creaking of wooden boards. Hellier was out of his chair and half way to the door when the thin screen moved back jerkily. A man squatted in the opening, blinking at the light and drawing deep breaths.

'Don't move,' he said softly. 'Don't either of you move.'

He squatted there like a toad, checking the room. He wore a sports shirt in thick black and white stripes, dark slacks with a wide leather belt; he was dirty and unshaven; thick black hair and dark sunken eyes.

Clumsily and with much caution and grunting he eased himself further into the room, sliding himself along on the seat of his slacks, not using his left leg at all, just propping himself on his left hand. In his right hand there was a gun.

'You the only two?' He spoke to Hellier.

'Yes. What do you want?'

The man edged himself so that he sat with his back to the wall beside the door; he shut the screen behind him. Now they could see his left leg, the ugly dark swelling above his sock where it had rolled down to his shoe, and they could smell the dried sweat.

'Broken ankle?' said Hellier.

'Maybe. Hurts like hell. You sure there's

64

nobody else here?'

'See for yourself,' said Hellier.

'Don't act smart with me, I'm not in the mood.'

'You need help,' said Hellier. He turned to Eileen Dempster. 'Would there be anything in the bathroom we could use? Bandages?'

She nodded, her eyes fixed on their visitor, and he gazed back with interest at her. 'Listen,' he said, 'you go get anything we need, okay, but remember if you try anything your boy friend here gets it in the belly.' He had the gun levelled at Hellier's middle. 'Don't come any nearer, mac, that's far enough.'

Eileen backed off, turned and went through to the bathroom, and presently they heard her running a tap in the basin.

'You better hope she's sensible,' said the man.

'You're a fool,' said Hellier. 'Where would she go? Who are you?'

'I'll need some chow when she gets back.' The man rubbed his hand over his mouth and jaw; his dirty skin was blotched and reddened and rough, swollen with insect bites, his forearms and the backs of his hands showed coarse dark hair matted with sweat. There was caked slime on his clothes. He was really rank and quite unsavoury.

'Be our guest,' said Hellier. 'Mind if I sit down?'

The man didn't say anything, so Hellier took a chair, the nearest chair, in full view.

'Give you one in the belly as soon as look at you,' the man said.

'Of course,' said Hellier. 'Just as you did to Edward Dempster.'

The man put his head on one side, pursed his lips, shook his head very slowly.

'He pulled a gun on me. What was I supposed to do? Laugh it off? You figure it.'

Eileen Dempster came in, her arms loaded. She knelt beside the man and put down the bowl of water; she had bandages, lint.

'I won't hurt you any more than I have to,' she said. 'I know something about first aid.'

'You better be good, lady.' The man held the gun so that its stubby barrel almost touched her face.

'Put that stupid thing away,' she said. 'It annoys me.'

Hellier watched with interest while the gun was withdrawn. But the man kept his hand on it. Eileen took out scissors and slit the laces of the man's shoe and very gently drew the shoe off, then peeled the sock away. The ankle was hideously swollen, the skin tight and shining, blue and dirty pale green.

She probed the swollen area with the tips of her fingers. The examination must have been painful, even though she was being so careful. The man made no sound. Only the hard set of his jaws showed what he was enduring.

'I don't think there's anything broken,' she said. She nursed the swollen foot in her lap and looked at the man.

'How did you do it?'

'I had a fall.'

She lowered her head and began sponging the dirt away from his foot while the man took a number of deep and noisy breaths.

'I'll fix up a compress with some ice cubes,' she said. 'That may help to bring the swelling down, and you'll have to stay off it … you've probably torn some ligaments in that ankle, and they won't mend in a hurry. Does it hurt much?'

The man was watching Hellier as he spoke. 'Nothing I can't take.'

'Good.' Eileen got to her feet. 'I'll get the ice.'

When she had gone, and they could hear her moving around in the kitchen, Hellier said quietly: 'You ought to feel like a right bastard – that's his wife, that's Mrs Dempster … she ought to let your blasted foot rot!'

'Mrs Dempster, eh? Too bad. He didn't say she was here – that makes it kind of complicated.'

'But nothing you can't handle I'm sure,' said Hellier heavily.

67

'That's right. I'm Kramer. You never heard tell of me, but you will, buddie boy, you will.'

'Paranoia. Did you have a deprived childhood as well? What brought you here? It wasn't just to kill Edward Dempster and Ahen Toong?'

'That the fat little spic? Never did get round to his name. Spunky little guy, tried to run out on me. But he didn't run so good. Messy.'

'It was,' said Hellier. 'Why didn't you just shoot him?'

'I had a problem,' said Kramer. 'There was this Dempster, I didn't want to scare him off too soon. Anyway, it didn't do no good because he lit out for the beach ... but I was up there with him by the time he got the engines going, and I just had to invite myself aboard. You getting the picture?'

'I think so,' said Hellier.

'He sure was no sailor, nor me. It was crazy, real crazy. We were heading out all over the place and he wouldn't stop... I figure he was off his head. Then he ran us slap-bang on those rocks. Knocked me ass over tea kettle. The next thing I know he's heading for the saloon and when I catch up with him he's got this little rod ... so he had to have it. Nothing else I could do.'

Eileen entered, carrying a muslin sling filled with the ice cubes. From her face there was no way of telling how much she had heard. She knelt down again.

'This ought to help,' she said and gently wound the ice pack round the swollen ankle, then swathed the pack loosely in bandages.

'Over on the couch,' she said. 'You'll be more comfortable there. Lean on me.'

She helped him to his feet with one of his arms around her shoulders. Hellier didn't stir as he watched them move, Kramer hopping on one foot, the gun dangling from his hand. When Kramer had been settled on the couch, one cushion under his damaged foot, she wiped her hands down the sides of her skirt and stood back.

'I don't ever want to touch you again.' Her voice was very soft and even and clear. 'As soon as you crawled in here I knew what you were and what you had done ... now I've heard it from your own lips, and I don't want to be near you again.'

'It was him or me,' said Kramer. 'Be reasonable, lady, he had the drop on me. I couldn't take any chances, so I had to let him have it. With a guy like that, there was no way of figuring what he'd do next.'

'You could have handled him without killing him,' said Hellier. 'You're some kind of a hired assassin, aren't you?'

Kramer looked at him. 'You're sounding off too loud, mac. I don't like it.'

'So what are you going to do about it?'

Hellier had got up from his chair.

Immediately Kramer had him covered with the gun, and it was clearly no idle move. 'One more step and you lose a kneecap. Like to try?'

'No, James,' whispered Eileen, 'don't–'

'Better listen to the lady.' Kramer's voice was quiet and unemphatic. 'There's no percentage in trying to act tough with me. Mebbe I got a busted ankle, but I don't shoot with my feet, and I couldn't miss you, not from here.'

Hellier relaxed, but remained standing. 'It won't be like this for long,' he said. 'When the time comes I'll be very happy to ram that gun down your dirty throat.'

Kramer smiled. 'That's my boy. Now here's the way it's going to be – one of you two is going to be right here with me all the time, and if anything happens that I don't like – suppose one of you gets the crazy idea of lighting out for the jungle, well, the one with me gets it – okay? No fooling. Now the lady can start by rustling me up some chow.'

'He's hungry,' said Hellier. 'Isn't that distressing?'

'He can starve for all I care.' Eileen turned on her heel.

'Hey you!' Kramer raised his voice at her. She went on. Into a bedroom.

Before Hellier had taken a step forward, Kramer lifted the gun and fired through the

70

ceiling. The room was still echoing with the explosion and the plaster was falling from the hole in the ceiling. Kramer had the gun back to cover Hellier.

'Like I told you,' he said. 'No fooling.'

'The point is well taken,' said Hellier. Eileen Dempster stood by the open door-way, rigid, her hand over her mouth. Blue smoke drifted in the light.

'Do I eat?' said Kramer.

Woodenly Eileen moved across to the kitchen, unable to take her eyes from the gun.

'It's all right,' said Hellier. 'Let him have something. If you find any strychnine in the larder shove it in his coffee.'

Kramer rotated his neck to ease his aching muscles. 'I always did like a guy with a sense of humour.'

'Big of you,' said Hellier.

Kramer stared at him. 'Just so long as he doesn't let it get ahead of him, mac.'

'One must keep things in proportion,' Hellier agreed politely.

'That's right. So you can sit where I can see you, like you were.' Kramer nodded at Eileen. 'And we'll have that door open. I'm going to hear what you're doing even when I don't see you. Okay? Don't make it too long.'

'Perhaps you'd like me to make you a drink?' said Hellier. 'It would be no trouble, and we do want you to feel at home.'

'Stay put. You talk too much.'

For a moment Eileen was looking at Kramer, her mouth very small and tight. Then she went into the kitchen without saying a word, and she left the door wide open. Hellier had resumed his seat.

'You won't be able to keep this up, you know,' he said. 'You'll make a mistake, and then I promise you it won't be a sprained ankle you'll be worrying about.'

Kramer jiggled the gun up and down gently, like a teacher making a point in the classroom with a stick of chalk. 'You don't look so dangerous from where I sit.'

Hellier smiled, and he had never felt less like smiling. 'Just one little mistake,' he said. 'That's all I need. It'll happen.'

'You won't live that long.' Kramer's smile matched his, and was probably genuine. 'You're on a licking to nothing, mac. You thought of that? I've taken care of two of them. So what makes you think it's going to be different for you, and her?'

'I have it in mind,' said Hellier. 'You operate wholesale.'

'Why not?' said Kramer. 'It make no kind of difference to me. Only three of us here, and I don't aim for you to get in my way.'

Chapter Six

They could hear Eileen moving around in the kitchen. Kramer shifted his leg into a more comfortable position on the cushion. 'She won't take off into the bush,' he said.

'If you'd put that gun away,' said Hellier, 'maybe we could make a bit more sense.'

'Not a chance. Put yourself in my place, with a busted leg and all. Where do you fit into this setup? I don't have your name yet – you come over with her?'

'Later. She was here when I arrived this afternoon. James Hellier. I was going to work for Dempster.'

Kramer smiled, his shoulders shook. 'You don't have much luck.'

'It varies,' said Hellier. 'You never know what's coming next ... how did you damage your foot?'

'Climbing those goddam cliffs, after I paddled back in that rubber thing. I must have come down fifty feet.'

'You should have made a proper job of it,' said Hellier. 'You could have broken your neck.'

'Pretty damn near did. I'm no goat. I reckon it took me close on three hours to get back on top. I been laying up in the bush all day. I saw you, you and her. I could've plugged the pair of you. You're not so smart. I saw you in the water – she's got a nice shape on her.'

Leaning forward in his chair, and keeping his voice low, Hellier said: 'You made her a widow, just a few hours ago. Don't you think you've done enough to her?'

'Make a good lay,' said Kramer. 'You some kind of a preacher?'

'Shut up!'

'Keeping it for yourself, mac? That the idea? Okay, okay, don't get yourself in a hassle.'

'If you touch her,' said Hellier in a whisper, 'you'll need more than one gun to keep me off.'

Kramer grinned, his teeth white against the dirt and stubble on his face. 'I can get a lay any time I want.'

'Not this time, not here. Stick to your killing.' Hellier rubbed the palms of his hands down his slacks. 'You'll have to sleep some time, I'll get you then if you've laid a hand on her.'

'I been sleeping most of the day,' said Kramer. 'Nothing else I could do in that jungle until it cooled off … you keep your woman, I don't reckon she'll do you much good.'

'Now you can shut up about it,' said

Hellier. 'What kind of an animal are you?'

Kramer's grin was lazy and full of confidence. 'And you're loaded with mush. All that heat over a woman beats me.'

'It would,' said Hellier.

Kramer dropped the gun into his lap and stretched, but his eyes didn't leave their target. He was willing Hellier to make a move.

'No?' he said softly.

'Not yet,' said Hellier. 'Tell me, how long have you been here on the island? How did you get here?'

'Like I told you before, you talk too much. If it makes you feel any happier, I been here since first light, and I got here same as you did, in a boat. Okay?'

Eileen came in with a tray. She put it on a low table near the couch and moved the table so that Kramer could reach it. Cold meat, bread, fruit, and a pot of coffee.

He told her where she was to sit, beside Hellier. 'You can watch the animal feed,' he said. 'Coffee smells good.'

So side by side they sat and watched, while Kramer had his meal, and, surprisingly enough, he proved to be a neat and fastidious eater. Hellier had expected to see him shovel the stuff down, but it was nothing like that. Nobody said anything, and when Hellier glanced at Eileen he saw that her eyes were fixed on the carpet beyond the couch; she might have been miles away.

When he had finished Kramer put the tray on the table. 'I'll have something to smoke,' he said. 'What have you got?'

Without a word Eileen got up and brought over the box of cigarettes and put them on the table.

'You can do better than that,' said Kramer. 'Your old man liked Havanas.'

'They're in the other room,' she said.

'Go get them.' Kramer grinned up into Eileen's face. He watched her cross the room. 'Not bad,' he murmured. 'For her age, not bad at all.'

'You didn't come here just for the purpose of killing Dempster,' said Hellier. 'I don't believe that – what did you come here for?'

'It wouldn't do you any good to know, so you can quit pestering me.' Eileen came back and put a box of cigars on the table beside the cigarettes.

'You wouldn't care for a liqueur?' she asked icily. 'We would hate you to feel neglected.'

Kramer selected a cigar with the un-hurried air of a man who knew what he was doing. 'I'll be needing some clean duds,' he said. 'Pants and shirt, socks.' He lit the cigar.

For a moment Eileen glanced appealingly at Hellier. He smiled. 'Treat it as a game,' he said quietly. 'It won't be for long, and he knows it ... we embarrass him by being here and knowing what he has done, because he doesn't know how soon they'll be coming for us.'

Kramer listened, his head on one side, the fragrant smoke wreathing his head. Eileen took a deep breath. 'All right,' she said. 'I'll get what he wants.'

Hellier sat back and crossed his legs. 'I could use one of those cigarettes.'

Kramer picked up the box and tossed it into his lap. 'I'll call your bluff,' he said. 'Who's coming for you and her? Nobody.'

'My dear man,' said Hellier, 'use your head, Mrs Dempster wasn't expecting to spend the night here, you didn't bring any luggage and neither did she. She was the wife of an important man in these parts, she'll be missed, they'll come looking for her here, it's obvious ... so you haven't a hope in hell of getting away with this. You're stuck.'

Kramer said nothing, just gave his attention to the ash on his cigar; he appeared no more thoughtful than his digestive operations might require; it was impossible to guess how much he had believed.

'You've backed yourself into a corner,' said Hellier, 'and you know it. Maybe wholesale killing doesn't bother you, but if you kill the two of us as well ... what happens when they come here looking for Mrs Dempster? You can't fake up any story to cover that. They'll see the boat, that's the first thing they'll start on, and you won't be able to explain that or the body there. I'd say you're cooked.'

Kramer went on placidly smoking. Occasionally he passed one hand over his tangled hair in a bored fashion, but he offered nothing in reply. Eileen returned with some clothes.

'In the bathroom, then come back here,' said Kramer. 'I want to talk to you.'

When she was sitting again he said: 'Your old man made a will? You'd know that, wouldn't you?'

'Of course,' she said stiffly. 'Why shouldn't I know that? My husband was a business man.'

'So who gets the loot now? You?'

She stared at him. 'I suppose so, if that's any concern of yours.'

'It could be,' he said.

'You murdered her husband,' said Hellier softly. 'Aren't you treating murder rather lightly?'

'Didn't have much choice, I told you... I'm thinking of a straight business proposition, with the lady–'

'You must be quite mad,' said Eileen, leaning forward in her chair.

'You haven't heard what it is yet,' said

Kramer. 'Maybe I'll tell you later, right now I want to clean up. Now both of you listen – we're all going into the bathroom, you in front and keep in sight, see? I'll be leaning on the lady and I'll have this gun in her ribs, so don't make me nervous. Okay? On your feet, give me a hand, and when I say stop we all freeze right there.'

He motioned with the gun and Hellier stood up and moved towards the bathroom door, just a few paces in front of the other two; Kramer had one arm around Eileen's shoulders, and the gun was just where he had promised it would be – but for that Hellier was sure he could have done something, but the gun cancelled it out.

'Put on the light and shift clear of the basin,' said Kramer. Then to Eileen: 'You sit in there and think about things … and don't do anything fancy while we're inside, because I'm getting good and sick of this guy and I might bop him – you read me loud and clear?'

Inside the bathroom Kramer hopped agilely across to the basin. 'Back up against that wall there,' he said to Hellier, 'and stay there.'

The gleaming length of the bath was between them. Kramer sat on a stool and propped his injured foot on the bath, sitting sideways so that he faced Hellier. He pulled off his tattered shirt with one hand; his body was brown and muscular and hairy, with a long pink scar running down into his belly. He ran hot water into the basin and took up Hellier's shaving brush. He had put the gun on the shelf just above the basin and near to his hand. He began to lather his chin.

'Now I know you're insane,' said Hellier. 'A business proposition – what possible business could you have with Mrs Dempster? You're having delusions, you stayed too long in the sun out there ... this is quite the daftest thing I ever heard – what is your business apart from murder?'

Kramer used Hellier's razor deftly and quickly. 'Nobody lives for ever ... no, don't move, buddie – unless you want me to spread you over that wall.'

Hellier resumed his position. 'You can't afford to kill me,' he said.

Kramer laughed a little, sponged his face and dried it. 'Now who's having the delusions?'

'Listen,' said Hellier. 'Exactly what do you want? What did you come here for?'

'And what makes you think I have to tell you?'

'Now you're just being coy,' said Hellier. 'It doesn't suit you. Who sent you here and why? Are you sure you came to the right place? There's nothing here for a man like you–'

'Correction,' said Kramer smiling and

80

running fresh water into the basin. 'You don't know what kind of a guy I am. You don't know anything. Period. So let's button it up... I could use a shower but I suppose that's expecting too much of a guy like you.'

'If that's a question,' said Hellier pleasantly, 'you know the answer – I'd like to see you take a shower on one foot and with a gun in your hand, I don't think I could resist it.'

Kramer got off the stool, undid his belt and wriggled out of his dirty slacks, then his pants.

'Charming,' said Hellier.

Standing on one leg, Kramer sponged himself with his left hand; he appeared to be enjoying himself; he had strong legs, slightly bowed, and very hairy.

'What a revolting sight,' said Hellier. 'You're making a mess on the floor.'

'Too bad. She can clean it up.'

'The manners of a pig and the appearance of an ape, you're really handicapped, aren't you?'

'I get by,' said Kramer cheerfully. 'You trying to needle me? Because you can save it.' He dried himself sketchily with one hand. 'Right here and now I reckon I'm the most important thing in your life and don't you forget it for one little minute.'

'As you profoundly remarked just now, nobody lives for ever – you'll never get yourself into those trousers without help, why not let me give you a hand?'

'You keep trying, bud, I'll say that for you ... if I get stuck I'll call in the little lady.'

'Bastard,' said Hellier nicely, and didn't move. The right time had come. Not yet, but soon, very soon he promised himself.

Kramer hauled on the slacks Eileen had left for him; they were baggy and dark brown, part of the wardrobe of the late Ahen Toong; there was also a khaki shirt with pockets and short sleeves, and Kramer didn't bother to do up the buttons. He sat on the stool and took off the one remaining shoe and sock, wiped his grimed foot on the towel and stood up on one leg.

'All fit,' he said. 'You first, and don't ruin yourself on the way.' He took the gun from the shelf. His face was shining. He seemed to be moving with more ease now. Hopping out of the bathroom just a few paces behind Hellier until he reached the back of a chair to lean on, then he made for the couch on his own and sat down, all the time covering Hellier. Eileen Dempster wasn't in the room.

'I'll get her,' said Hellier.

'You'll get nothing but a slug in the belly if you don't sit,' said Kramer.

'She's had enough,' said Hellier. 'Let her sleep, you don't have to put on your tough act with her, work it off on me.'

'Sure, sure,' said Kramer. 'So I had to knock off her old man and that makes everybody sad all round.'

'You're an animal, nothing more and nothing less.'

'I'm the guy with the gun,' said Kramer. 'That makes me different.'

Eileen had heard their voices, she appeared in the doorway, and without looking at Kramer she said: 'I'm going to bed.'

'We'll all use the same room,' said Kramer.

Slowly Eileen turned her head to look at him with open contempt. 'I'll lock myself in, I won't have you in the same rom. You understand? I won't.'

'Have to shoot the lock off ... all in the one room. So as I can see both of you all the time.' He grinned at her. 'You don't have to worry, there'll be nobody shacking up with you, lady ... not unless you insist.'

'I'd rather be dead,' she said.

'Listen,' said Kramer, and for the first time he seemed impatient, 'I got bigger things on my mind right now than a quick lay, so you can forget it – we use the same room, and I don't reckon to be doing any sleeping.'

'You'd better not,' said Hellier, 'or you'll wake up in a mess. It's all right, Eileen, we'll humour him, nothing's going to happen, he's just nervous, that's what this is all

83

about, a fit of the jitters.'

'You keep thinking on those lines,' said Kramer. He stuffed the box of cigars inside the front of his shirt. 'Leave all the lights. Anybody wants to use the bathroom can have three minutes, after that we shut the place up, okay?'

The larger of the two bedrooms had twin beds. Kramer switched on the fan in the ceiling and told Hellier to make sure that the screen was down over the wide window, and watched him while he did it. Kramer had some cushions on the floor so that he sat with his back against the door and facing the two beds; he had lit another cigar, and the gun lay on a cushion beside his hand.

Eileen had taken off her shoes. She gave Hellier a little smile. 'It's quite ridiculous,' she murmured. 'Good night, James.'

She turned to face the wall, and the fan flip-flopped gently overhead. Hellier sat up with the pillows at his back and his hands linked behind his head. Kramer met his glance and waved the end of his cigar.

'Settle down, mac,' he said. 'Let the lady sleep. I got everything under control.'

Hellier smiled. 'Like to bet you fall off first?'

'You're out of your league,' said Kramer. 'You wouldn't live to collect. Now button it up.'

Outside the night wind rustled the palms. Blue cigar smoke rose and swirled about in the fan. Kramer was absolutely still, watching the window behind Hellier's head, where suicidal insects pinged against the screen. Eileen appeared to be sleeping, at last. The single light was on the dressing-table and well out of Hellier's reach.

For over two hours he maintained his vigil, and whenever he made any move he was aware of Kramer's eyes on him. He had no clear memory of falling asleep, it just crept over him, and then defeated him.

The sound of men's voices roused him just before dawn. He got up on one elbow. Kramer was already on one foot, the gun in his hand.

'You lost your bet, mac,' he said. He opened the door and hopped out.

Chapter Seven

There was a thumping of boots on the wooden veranda, and the door was thrust open violently. Four men came in – two young men with carbines who immediately separated and took up positions on each side of the door; they wore grey-green denims, combat boots, and peaked caps, no badges; they looked very young and serious, and a little out of breath. The third one wore a similar outfit, but with a belt, and he had a revolver, and a better cap with a badge. All three were natives.

The fourth man was very different. Much older, and unarmed. He wore a rumpled tussore suit and a faded yellowing straw hat. A tall stooping man, with a white moustache fringed with tobacco stains, and a high beaky nose. He had a much lighter skin than the others, but wrinkled and dry, there was no shine on it at all; his bushy eyebrows were darker than his moustache.

'Right on the dot, Ramon,' said Kramer, sounding very pleased. 'Nice timing, chief.'

Ramon stared past him, looking at Hellier in the doorway.

'Who is this one?' He had a soft voice,

polite – but the voice of a man who is in the habit of getting the right answers.

'Nobody who matters to us,' said Kramer and hopped further into the room. 'Strictly zero, that one.'

'Who is it?' Ramon ignored Kramer's disability.

'I happened to turn up here at the wrong time for somebody, it seems,' said Hellier. 'And for that matter, who the hell are you lot? Why the guns?'

Ramon began to saunter slowly around the room, like a bailiff who is about to distrain on the property and sees little of value.

'An untidy situation,' he said. 'Where is Dempster?'

'There was a little difficulty,' said Kramer.

'He's dead,' said Hellier harshly, and he knew that Eileen had come to stand behind him. 'Murdered, and so was his servant ... he did it – ask him, he killed both of them.' Hellier came away from the doorway and into the room, at last he felt he had some attention.

Ramon pursued his lips, the stained moustache outthrust. He didn't look at Kramer, just remained in a thoughtful pose.

'Listen,' said Kramer. He had found a chair, and he might have looked happier if somebody had noticed his injury; he still held his gun loosely in his hand. 'You just wait until you hear how it was, chief. You know me, you know I wouldn't have done it if there had been any other way, but there wasn't.'

'Indeed? You sold yourself to me as a professional, an amateur could have handled it better. He was not to be killed. I made that plain.' Ramon pulled at his thin nose with finger and thumb. Now he noticed Eileen, and he took his time about it. 'Who is this?'

'Mrs Dempster,' said Hellier. 'Dempster's widow–'

'Unfortunate, very unfortunate. Madam, my condolences.' Ramon lifted his straw hat perfunctorily, showing close-cropped white hair, very strong and coarse. 'This was no part of my instructions, I would have preferred to find your husband alive.'

'That's nice of you,' said Hellier. 'I suppose that makes it all right? What the hell do you think you're running here? If this hoodlum is under your orders I don't think much of your organization–'

'See what I mean?' said Kramer to Ramon. 'He belly-aches all the time. He talks real tough. We ought to be taking care of him, he says he was going to work for Dempster–'

'Take the woman away,' said Ramon. 'Look after her, I will see her later, put her in a room alone.'

One of the young guards with a carbine

shoved Hellier out of the way, not too gently, and escorted Eileen out of the room. Hellier watched her go and felt absolutely helpless. The officer-type with the cap and the revolver was smiling at him and shaking his head slightly. There were more men outside on the veranda. This was an armed invasion, no less.

'Now Kramer,' said Ramon, 'where is the body? What have you done with it? Show it to me.'

'I didn't have much chance to tidy up,' Kramer began sulkily.

'He means you'll find the body on Dempster's cruiser,' said Hellier. 'Wrecked on the reef, up off the north coast–'

'What the hell difference does it make?' Kramer burst out angrily.

'And the wreck can be seen?' said Ramon.

'In daylight you can't miss it,' said Hellier. 'The first aircraft to pass this way in the morning will report it, don't you make any mistake.'

'There is no regular air route anywhere near here,' said Ramon.

'They'll be searching for Dempster, and his wife,' said Hellier. 'He was due in Antigua tomorrow, Mrs Dempster was going to Jamaica ... there'll be a search all right.'

'I hoped you understood my instructions,' said Ramon to Kramer. 'Nothing of this was

90

to happen.'

Kramer sat there and shrugged. 'It blew up,' he said. 'Dempster wouldn't listen–'

'It was your mission to hold him here until I arrived and talked to him,' said Ramon. 'I warned you he could not be bullied, that there was to be no strong-arm business, so you shoot him. Who else is here apart from the woman and this man?'

'Nobody,' said Kramer. 'I damn near broke my leg–'

'My felicitations. It was foolish of me to let you work on your own, now we must do what we can to repair the damage you have done.'

'I don't see what the beef is all about,' said Kramer. 'The place is all ours, right? That's what you wanted.'

Hellier had been watching the young officer with the revolver, noting the very careful movements he had been making that brought him close to where Kramer sat.

'The position I find here is not at all what I planned or wanted,' said Ramon. 'Using you was my mistake, and that is one mistake that I am now able to rectify.'

'You'd better ease off that stuff and listen to me,' said Kramer.

Perhaps Ramon gave some kind of a signal to the young officer, if he did Hellier quite missed it, but the officer moved with surprising speed, bending over Kramer and holding him down in his chair, one hand pinning the gun in Kramer's fist so that it was useless. Kramer swore, stiffening his body, the officer brought his boot squarely down on Kramer's damaged foot. There was a squeal of pain, and Kramer let his gun slip to the floor, and the officer kicked it out of reach.

Kramer's face was twisted and shining with sweat, trembling he was reaching down to his aching ankle. The officer clubbed his revolver and hit Kramer flush on the temple and caught him before he began to fall.

Keeping fastidiously well clear of the encounter, Ramon nodded. 'Dispose of him outside,' he said. 'I have no more use for him.'

The remaining guard moved smartly forward and took Kramer's shoulders, and helped the officer to remove the useless one, kicking the screen door open. Kramer's gun lay on the floor just a few feet from where Hellier was standing. He looked at it, just looked at it, and found Ramon's gaze on him, a very penetrating and steady gaze.

'You would accomplish nothing but your own speedy dissolution,' said Ramon softly. 'We are not alone.'

From the open door another guard covered him, and in the darkness beyond could be heard the agonized pleadings of Kramer's shrill voice, fading now and rising to nothing. Then the one sharp explosion.

Hellier found his mouth suddenly dry. 'More killing,' he said.

'Execution,' said Ramon.

'Who are you? God? He was a murderer … but are you any better?'

The guard in the door cleared his throat. All he wanted was just one little sign from the chief; the pink tip of his tongue moistened his lips; one blast of that carbine at that close range would slice James Hellier in half.

'You are a man of sense,' said Ramon. 'Why be unrealistic? There is nothing you can hope to do in this situation. As the un-lamented Kramer put it, you are a zero … it would be foolish not to recognize that, and you are not a fool, I think.'

'Put it in writing and I'll have it framed.'

'I have yet to hear your name,' said Ramon.

'James Hellier, if it matters. And you, I take it, must be some kind of a local bandit chief – your intelligence section let you down badly this time, there's nothing to steal here.'

Ramon's face tightened; his thin nostrils spread. His voice was still gentle, but very emphatic. 'You should not say that in front of my people, they would consider it an insult, and you would not live much longer. I could do nothing to protect you.'

'All right then,' said Hellier. 'So you're

legitimate. You're not a comic opera bandit, so why the flock of armed underlings? You hired Kramer to do some kind of a job here and he fell down on it, so you've just had him shot. And you haven't seemed exactly heart-broken over the murder of Dempster and his servant – forgive me if I appear a little out of touch, but I have old fashioned ideas about cold blooded killing ... and I find you a little too strong for my stomach.'

'You mean you are frightened,' said Ramon. 'That is reasonable.'

'I mean that I have seen nothing so far to persuade me that you're not the boss of a band of thugs.'

'It is all in the point of view,' said Ramon pleasantly. 'One should always keep in mind the greatest good of the greatest number. Emergencies make their own rules.'

'I must remember to pass that profound thought on to Mrs Dempster,' said Hellier. 'It will comfort her enormously.'

'We intend no harm to her, or you, if you continue to be sensible. It is a pity you are both here, but since you are–'

'We are both ready to leave any time you give the word,' said Hellier. 'I suppose you have some kind of a boat down there in the bay, just put us aboard and drop us off where it's half-way civilized–'

'Not yet,' said Ramon. 'That is not possible.'

'Why?'

'It is futile to discuss it,' said Ramon. 'There are more important considerations—'

The guard at the door was pushed aside and a girl strode in. She wore tight khaki slacks and a khaki bush shirt; a belt with a holster tugged at her narrow waist; she had thick dark hair cut short, a wide full mouth, and a neat finely featured face. She appeared to be about twenty. Lively, radiating energy.

She looked at Hellier. 'Well,' she said, 'so this is the one. He looks okay to me.' She turned to Ramon and said: 'I see you finally got round to Kramer, didn't I warn you he was wrong for it, didn't I?'

'You did,' said Ramon.

'Well then.' The girl flung herself into a chair and let her legs sprawl; she unhooked her belt and let it drop to the floor and the holster made a clunk on the soft carpet. She ran both hands through her thick hair, lifting her breasts under the thin shirt. 'There's a woman, they tell me, where is she?'

'In one of the bedrooms, there is a guard with her.'

'Good,' said the girl. She smiled at Hellier and nodded. 'Your woman, perhaps?'

'No.' Hellier was standing. He sat down. The girl went on examining him without reticence; an expert appraisal; while Ramon just stood by her chair as though reluctant

95

to intervene, a thin indulgent smile on his face.

'He's an improvement on that ape Kramer,' she said. 'He looks healthy enough.'

'I couldn't have put it better myself,' said Hellier, and her gaze shifted and went right over his head – he might have been an item of furniture that had met with her approval.

'Esmée,' said Ramon quietly, touching her shoulder.

She stretched and his hand dropped away; her smile became wider than ever, showing tiny pointed teeth; a female shark, savouring her own reverie. Inelegantly she scratched in the pit of one arm.

'I'm crawling,' she said. 'That lousy boat of yours was alive, Ramon … is there a bathroom in this place?'

'We have every amenity,' said Hellier. 'May I show you?'

She brought her gaze back to him; she laughed. 'A comedian! How's your health and strength, mister?'

'Now Esmée,' said Ramon. 'There is no time for any of that…'

'There is always time,' she said lazily. 'You are too old, you have forgotten – if you were not my uncle I would revive your memory.'

The young officer with the revolver and the peaked cap had returned, looking pleased with himself after attending personally to the matter of the unlucky Kramer.

There was a touch of swagger in his style as he crossed the room so that Esmée could see what a fine figure he made. All present and correct, one hand still on the holster, unbuttoned. She didn't spare him a glance.

Ramon indicated Hellier in the chair. 'Put him with the woman,' he said. Esmée's breasts jiggled as she laughed and threw her arms wide as though to embrace an unseen lover. Hellier could feel her eyes on him as he allowed himself to be taken out.

'What quaint ideas you still have, Ramon,' said Esmée. 'What possible damage could I do to him? A big strong man like that? It tones the system up, or have you forgotten that as well? Poor Uncle Ramon! How dull your world must be.'

Hellier was wishing he could wait to hear Ramon's comment, but his escort was being efficient with his gun in the small of Hellier's back.

They had put Eileen in Toong's little room, in the rear beside the kitchen; the guard was squatting on the floor with the door open and his carbine between his knees. Eileen sat on the edge of the narrow bed, her hands loose in her lap, while the sorrowing Christ gazed down on her from the Cross. She looked quite desolate and weary.

'You will both remain in here until we send for you,' said the officer importantly.

'There doesn't appear to be any alternative,' said Hellier.

'It will do you no good to be insolent,' said the officer.

'Who was the nympho out there? Friend of yours? She ought to be doctored.' For a second Hellier thought the young officer was going to hit him with his gun; the young man's face had darkened, and his jaw had clamped hard. Then he turned on his heel, whispered something to the guard who still squatted on the floor, and marched out.

Hellier sat beside Eileen. 'I'm afraid it hasn't got any better,' he said mildly. 'There's a whole army of them.'

She shuddered, and he put an arm around her. 'It'll be all right,' he said.

The guard hawked noisily and spat into the corridor. Grinned at them and made the universal obscene gesture, his carbine held between his knees.

Hellier started to rise, but Eileen held him back. 'No,' she said, 'what's the use? It wouldn't help.'

The guard laughed. 'Pretty lady got sense,' he said.

In the greying light outside there seemed to be a number of men on the move, and some of them were carrying crates or boxes heavy enough to need two men; there was about them an air of quiet discipline – and haste; no laughing or chattering.

Eventually Hellier got up and went over to the small window to get a better view. The guard stirred and said sharply: 'You git clear away from that goddam window, you hear?'

'I hear.' Hellier resumed his place on the edge of the bed.

'Who are they?' said Eileen. 'What do they want here?'

'We've been invaded,' said Hellier. 'Did your husband ever dabble in politics?'

'It's very unlikely,' she said. 'He was far too busy making money.'

'Then I haven't a clue,' said Hellier. 'Not yet.'

Chapter Eight

Within an hour the young officer returned, jerked the guard to his feet and motioned him to station himself further along the corridor.

'I am Captain Esposito,' he said. 'You are to be in my charge. There will be no more insolence.' He was looking at Hellier as he spoke, and Hellier gave him a friendly grin.

'Anything you say, Captain.'

'We will be leaving soon,' said Esposito. 'You may each use the bathroom, if necessary.'

'Very humane,' said Hellier. 'Where are we going?'

Eileen went out. Esposito adopted a watchful at ease position; the guard was picking his nose; all the movement out there in the rear had stopped, and when Hellier took a quick look he saw nobody at all.

'Where are we going?' he asked again, and Esposito didn't even look at him. 'How did you get to be a Captain, old son? In which army?'

'I said no insolence.' Esposito barely opened his lips; the guard was listening and grinning hugely. 'That is an order.'

'You need a shave and a hair cut,' said Hellier, 'and those boots are a disgrace to the regiment, if you have a regiment, which I doubt.'

Captain Esposito swallowed audibly, and was happy to see Eileen emerged from the bathroom. 'You have two minutes, no more,' he said and Hellier went in, the guard following as far as the door.

When they were escorted through the living room Hellier noticed that it had been tidied, and there was no evidence that anybody had been using the room recently. They went out to the veranda and the morning light and the clear air.

'You will hurry,' said Esposito. 'Down to the beach. If there is any stupidity I will shoot the lady first. Understood?'

Again he was talking to Hellier. They seemed to have the place to themselves, and Hellier had been expecting some kind of a posse. It smelt good and fresh.

As they crossed the open space in front of the bungalow Hellier was wondering what they had done with Kramer's body. There was no sign of Ramon or the lady Esmée; it was as though none of them had ever been there. When the path sloped he took Eileen's arm and gave it a reassuring squeeze, and he was aware of Captain Esposito just a pace behind them.

He had some thoughts about trying a

quick turn and a slam at the Captain's gun, but then they had made the first turn, and it was no real surprise to see the ship down in the bay. When he hesitated momentarily he heard Eileen gasp and jerk as Esposito jammed his gun into the small of her back, and before he could turn Esposito had stepped back and was out of easy and safe reach, with the gun pointed at Eileen, as he had promised.

'All right,' said Hellier. 'Just don't be so free with the armoury.' So they went on down.

The ship was a dirty grey, a tramp, about a thousand tons, bluff in the bows, with plenty of beam, flying no flag that Hellier could see; oil burning; sturdy enough, a sister to most of the craft that plied their trade among the islands. A small boat was pulling back to the jetty.

'I suppose it's no good asking where you're taking us?' said Hellier.

'You suppose right,' said Esposito.

They reached the jetty at the same time as the boat; there were two oarsmen, not in any kind of a uniform; tough and seasoned seamen who showed no interest in the passengers beyond seeing that they were properly stowed in the stern; the six of them made a fair load, and the oarsmen took their time pulling back.

When Captain Esposito commanded

more speed one of the rowers told him what he could do with himself, and they continued at a steady and leisurely pace, without any light conversation. It could have been a pleasant trip, all the ingredients were there: bright sunshine coming through the morning mist, a flat clear sea, the greenery of the island moving away from them.

'You might have let us take a bit of luggage,' said Hellier. 'Why all the mad rush?'

'You will be comfortable enough,' said Esposito. 'We are not barbarians.'

'You could have fooled me,' said Hellier. 'What do you call that old tub there? Is that the best you could manage?'

'It serves our purpose.'

They came alongside and there was a rope ladder dangling for them, and some faces watching with open interest, especially at the sight of Eileen preparing to climb up. She followed Esposito, and Hellier came after her, and he made sure that the audience saw less than they had hoped. Esposito hustled them along the deck and down a companion, and the ship was already vibrating with the engines; there was the shipboard smell of paint and oil and old food. He slid back two doors at the after end.

'A cabin for each of you,' he said. 'You will not be locked in unless you make it necessary, there will be food brought for you and you will be permitted to use the deck up there for exercise ... you will not talk to the crew–'

'Understood,' said Hellier. 'A mystery tour, right?'

Captain Esposito smiled for the first time, but at Eileen.

'I regret we do not have stewardesses with us, we were not expecting to carry a lady.'

Eileen just shrugged, Esposito clicked his heels and went off, the holster slapping at his thigh.

'Kidnapped,' said Hellier. 'Which cabin would you like, Eileen?'

They examined the accommodation, two cabins of exactly the same size, tiny cupboards with a single bunk in each and a porthole and some hooks in place of wardrobes, a small square of stained carpet beside each bunk, a collapsible wooden flap bolted to a bracket to serve as a table. An exhibition of colourful nudes in highly improper postures had been pasted along the bulkhead in one of the cabins, so Eileen chose the other.

They were on the move. A youth in stained drill shorts and a tee shirt arrived with a tray; there were two mugs of coffee and some bread rolls and a slab of melting butter. Hellier took the tray. 'Good,' he said briskly, 'now ask the purser if he's got anything to smoke.'

'Sah?' The youth was very black and cheerful, stealing sideways looks at Eileen and pretending he was doing nothing of the kind; he had large bare feet.

'Cigarettes,' said Hellier.

The youth ducked his head, shuffled off, and looked back and giggled. At Eileen.

The coffee was all right. 'Let's take breakfast up on deck,' said Hellier. 'We might get some idea where they're taking us.'

When they arrived again in the sun they found their part of the deck deserted, everybody appeared to be for'ard; on the flying bridge they could see Ramon, with some men in peaked caps, all gazing for'ard. The ship was creeping slowly towards the reefs off the northern coast of the island. There was the wrecked cruiser still, on the coral, and a rowing boat stood by, clear of the reef.

Bells clanged in the engine room, the ship gently lost way, the flat sea slapping softly against her sides; the rowing boat backed and came out to meet them; there was some shouting up for'ard, and a rope snaked down and one of the rowers caught it, waved and the boat sidled back until it was a few feet from the cruiser.

Hellier had already guessed what they were doing, and he felt Eileen stiffen beside him at the rail, and when she turned away he let her go below. He saw the man clamber over the stern of the cruiser, heaving on the rope; he made it fast somewhere, and got back into the rowing boat. There was more waving and the rowing boat moved clear. Everybody watched.

The rope dipped and tightened with the harsh sound of a winch turning, the cruiser jerked and slid off the reef and down into the deep water, floating for some twenty or forty feet on an uneven keel, well down by the stern, clearly sinking. The rowing boat edged alongside, the rope was cast off and the cruiser rocked gently, tilted slightly and then went under. The rowing boat headed back. That took care of the funeral of Edward Dempster. And removed the wrecked cruiser from any inquisitive eyes.

The group on the bridge had begun to disperse. Hellier was sure Ramon had seen him at the rail, but he gave no sign, and presently he had disappeared.

Hellier waited for a while, alone at the rail. Eileen wouldn't be needing his company, and he knew very well he couldn't be any kind of a comfort to her, not yet. This was something she would want to cope with on her own, he thought he knew enough of her to be sure of that. She'd been taking a battering in the last few hours.

She had said she had wanted a divorce from Edward Dempster, but what had happened to him must have made her feel pretty bad, and he wondered if she would be ever wholly free of the memory of her husband, and the macabre way her freedom had come.

Freedom? An unpleasant joke all round. What good was freedom from an unhappy union going to be to her now? They were in the way. Both of them. This was going to be no pleasure cruise.

The rowing boat had now been swung inboard, and the beat of the engines had become pronounced; they were turning clear of the reefs and heading out into the open sea. Hellier watched the dark green shape of the island, slipping behind them now, losing height in the water. Ahen Toong's body lay rotting up there on the jungle slope; in the sunken cabin Edward Dempster's body would be bloated beyond recognition; what had they done with Kramer?

Who was going to be next? Whoever Ramon might be and whatever dirty business he might be engaged on, one thing was clear – he took a light-hearted view of human life. That gentle voice didn't mean a thing, or that air of middle-aged mildness. Not a man to have on the other side. Ramon Who? And from where?

Captain Esposito was coming smartly along the deck; his boots going snap-snap, nicely burnished; there was a powdered and newly shaven sheen on his jaw. He fetched up in front of Hellier, stiff and very correct; the corners of his mouth twitched, and his gaze was fixed on a point over Hellier's head. He might have been handing over the parade to the Commanding Officer.

'At ease, lad,' said Hellier, lounging comfortably against the rail. 'You'll do yourself an injury, stamping about the deck like that.'

'It amuses you to insult me,' said Esposito in a choked and quite unmilitary voice. 'In your position it is not wise.'

'The only weapon I have left,' said Hellier. 'Ridicule. It shouldn't bother you too much – you'd better put me on a charge, I could do with a few words with this chief of yours, Ramon, or whatever he calls himself. I have some questions I'd like answering.'

'You have nothing,' said Esposito. 'If Señor Ramon had taken the advice we have given him, you would not be smiling. You would be dropped over the side with chains about your feet.'

'A bit drastic.'

Esposito's mouth widened. 'You would find that ridiculous? You do not take us seriously.'

'Indeed I do. I'm not laughing.'

Some of the stiffness went out of Esposito's posture. 'You are an unlucky man.'

'You could be right,' said Hellier. 'So

what's the good news this time?'

'You were instructed not to talk with any of the crew.'

'Have a heart,' said Hellier. 'I need a cigarette to keep my morale up, and I expect Mrs Dempster does as well – does she have to share my bad luck?'

'You need discipline,' said Esposito. 'You are too flippant.'

Hellier spread his empty hands. 'Then just tell me how long this trip is going to last? Where are we heading now? Or haven't the bosses told you that much?'

'I obey orders.' It came out very pat. 'And you will do the same. Now you will go below and remain in your cabin.'

'Confined to barracks?' said Hellier. 'What are you all so scared of? Don't you trust your own crew, is that it?'

'You understand nothing,' said Esposito, 'and you will not co-operate.'

'You've been pushing us about ever since you arrived, I don't see what the hell you're complaining about.'

'You make this all a joke,' said Esposito stiffly.

'Not any more,' said Hellier. 'I don't know what you're up to, but I don't think it's at all funny, and neither does Mrs Dempster, you've all been acting like an illegal bunch of bastards–'

'That is enough.'

'Well what else would you expect us to think? You barge in bristling with guns and so forth, you shoot that thug Kramer, you don't show the slightest concern over what happened to Edward Dempster and his man, you offer no explanation – not a damn word, and we're supposed to accept it all as right and proper!'

'I have no information for you,' said Esposito.

'A joke!' said Hellier bitterly. 'We'd have to be a pair of morons to find anything funny in this. Does the embargo apply to Mrs Dempster? Is she forbidden to come up on deck? You can't be scared of her, surely?'

'I have no instructions about the lady. She may please herself, but you will not appear on deck until I tell you.'

'All right.' Hellier moved towards the head of the companionway, not hurrying, his hands in his pockets.

'Don't you think you're being just a little too sensitive about this?' he said.

'I have my orders. You are not trustworthy.'

'That's rich,' said Hellier, 'bearing all things in mind.'

'We could have disposed of the two of you last night,' said Esposito in a flat tone. 'It would have been simple.'

'I'm wondering why you didn't,' said Hellier.

'Señor Ramon is not what you are thinking. He is a great man, and he does not wish to have useless bloodshed.'

'You comfort me,' said Hellier. 'I'm glad he has some scruples, I only hope they are strong enough to take any strain you lot might put on them – would it be possible for me to express my sentiments to Señor Ramon in person?'

Captain Esposito had moved a little closer, now neither of them was in view of the bridge, and they had that small slice of the deck to themselves.

'One moment,' said Esposito. He was holding out an unopened packet of cigarettes. English Embassy in the familiar white wrapping with the thin scarlet stripe. There was also a booklet of matches. 'You should ask me for what you want,' he said.

Hellier took the cigarettes. 'Thanks,' he said. 'I misjudged you, I'm afraid.'

'You are a man without luck,' said Esposito.

'That sounds like my obituary.' Hellier balanced the packet of cigarettes on the palm of his hand; the sea was a flat and shining blue-green, and the island was a tiny lump of darkness on the horizon. 'What about Mrs Dempster? What are you going to do with her?'

'You both present the same problem,' said Esposito. 'Now you will go below and you will stay there. If you are needed I will come for you.' He waited until Hellier had gone below before moving off.

When Hellier found the door of Eileen's cabin closed he thought about knocking, then decided he had nothing helpful to tell her. Far from it. She would have enough on her mind.

He sat on the edge of his bunk and opened the cigarettes; everything was vibrating and there was plenty of engine noise below; he wrestled with the rusty fastening of the porthole and got it open after taking some skin off his knuckles and the small cabin began to smell better; the bunk had a striped bolster and pair of thin and not too clean blankets, but the mattress looked reasonable, so he threw the blankets to the foot of the bunk and settled himself down. There was absolutely nothing else to do. Except think. And that got him nowhere.

He had no idea of the time, his watch hadn't been going since the swim out to the wrecked cruiser, but he knew he was hungry again, and the cigarettes weren't helping much. After a while he tried to erase some of the more obscene of the nudes on the bulkhead, but they had been pasted on by an enthusiast and wouldn't respond. He spent some time kneeling up on the bunk and with his head out of the porthole; the breeze was refreshing, and he guessed they were making eight knots or so, and they seemed to have all that clear sea to themselves.

He dozed on the bunk, but the rumblings in his stomach roused him and he went out into the companionway. There were three doors opposite, two of them locked and the third was a bathroom of sorts, with a hand pump for the basin and the toilet, a small piece of off-white soap and a grimy towel on a hook behind the door.

When he emerged he met the youth with the tray, again, standing outside the closed door of Eileen's cabin. The youth looked a little unhappy. The tray had plates of salad with slices of thick pale ham, bananas and sliced water melon; there was another tall pot of coffee and bread rolls. The youth held out the tray and Hellier accepted it, and this time he did nothing but nod. The youth took off at speed and without a backward glance.

Hellier put the tray on his bunk and knocked on Eileen's door. 'Lunch is served.'

She was a little time answering, and when she came out she had been crying, and although she said she didn't want anything he made her go into the cabin and sat her down on the bunk.

'The menu is limited,' he said, 'but at least they don't intend us to starve. You'll find bathroom facilities across the way, primitive but adequate. Third door on your right.'

'I'd rather eat this on deck,' she said. 'Couldn't we?'

'You can,' he said. 'Not me. Captain Esposito has confined me to quarters, temporarily – I have contravened ship's standing orders by talking to the lad with the tray. Very serious. But I got us some cigarettes.'

'Then we'll both eat here,' she said.

'Nothing would please me better,' he said, and coaxed a weak smile out of her, which was a move in the right direction, he thought. Her face was shiny with sweat and her hair was tangled and damp.

'You wouldn't happen to have a comb about you I suppose?' she said wearily.

'Sorry.' He poured her a cup of coffee.

'Give me a couple of minutes to tidy myself.' She got up and went across to the bathroom.

To hell with Captain Esposito. Hellier made his way to the head of the companionway and shouted. The officer on watch on the flying bridge saw him and Hellier waved madly and shouted some more: 'Ahoy there, you miserable bastards! You wall-eyed sons of bitches, let's have some service back here!'

The officer cupped his hands and said: 'Bastard yourself. What you want?'

'Esposito, you fetch Esposito. And pretty damn quick!'

Chapter Nine

Captain Esposito came running, without his cap and looking very angry and ready to invoke all the martial law he might know. Hellier cut him short.

'Now you just listen to me for a moment,' he said. 'You call yourself civilized – and you can stick that bloody little gun back while I talk to you – you've got a lady on board and you didn't have the manners to allow her to bring any luggage, not even her handbag. Hell's bells, what kind of morons are you? She needs stuff, a comb at least, for Pete's sake, and you might rustle up a clean towel and some decent soap for that stinking little bathroom you expect us to use – you get the message, Captain? We think the service is lousy, we didn't ask to be shanghaied on to this dirty old tub, and now that you've got us here you'll have to pull your finger out. Okay?'

Captain Esposito was plainly disconcerted at the vehemence of the attack, and at its subject matter.

'The lady is not comfortable?' he said.

'You bet your sweet life,' said Hellier. 'So let's have a touch of the old Caribbean

117

courtesy. She's a lady, not a tramp – or wouldn't you know the difference?'

'I do what I can, you wait here – but no more of the rude shouting.'

'Not a peep,' said Hellier. 'Just bring the stuff, and on the double.'

A few minutes later he was knocking on the bathroom door. He had a pink plastic comb that looked new, a blue and white striped towel and a cake of new soap. When Eileen opened the door and peeped out he said: 'Compliments of the management.'

They had finished lunch, the youth had come for their tray, and Eileen had been up on deck for a few minutes on her own; they'd had some desultory conversation in which Hellier had admitted that he had tried in vain to get to Ramon.

'Negative all round,' he had said. 'Either Esposito doesn't know where they're taking us, or it's top secret. Take your pick. They seem to have a problem with us, simply because we were on the island, we get in their way.'

'I don't like the sound of that very much,' Eileen had said.

'There's another angle – if they had been going to do anything drastic to us why did they go to the trouble of marching us on to this boat? It doesn't add up, but I'm still optimistic – I wish I could get at that

Ramon character.'

The heat had increased, and even with the portholes open and the doors of the cabins wide there was little air moving. There were no fans, and the glare of the strong sunlight from the head of the companionway showed up all the blotched and dirty paintwork, and the incessant humming of the engines gave Eileen a headache, along with the stale air; her face was grey and dispirited, and Hellier had long run out of suitable small-talk.

He was snoozing on his bunk when the visitor arrived on silent feet to stand in the doorway. A tall and slender young man, wearing stained blue slacks and rope-soled sandals; he had no shirt and his chest was smooth and brown and hairless, like that of a boy; he had a long and knowing face, with a mouth that was too full and too red to be right for a man; he had lots of tight curly black hair, and rings on the fingers of both hands.

Right then from the start Hellier decided he didn't like the way the young man was looking at him and smiling. There was something distinctly unpleasant about the twist in that over-red mouth.

'*Compadre*,' said the young man, 'you come with me.'

Hellier slid to his feet. 'Where?'

The young man turned and sauntered off

119

down the companionway, past Eileen's open door, where he paused for a moment, because he was the kind of man who would instinctively halt at the sight of an attractive woman on a bed. Hellier came up behind him and shoved him out of the way, and his hand felt dirty where it touched that naked back.

Eileen was sitting up. 'I've been summoned into the presence at last,' said Hellier. 'I won't be long.'

'Ramon?' she said.

'I expect so.'

'I'm coming,' she said and got up off the bunk.

The young man was lounging against the bulkhead, his arms folded across his naked chest, a plainly lascivious grin on his face at the sight of Eileen.

'Ver' nice,' he said, 'but she is not wanted, only the Señor this time – you tell her.'

Eileen halted. 'Time for you mebbe later,' said the young man. 'You go catch yourself some sleep, *chiquita.*'

'Be careful what you say,' said Eileen. 'Please.'

'I will,' said Hellier.

He followed the young man up into the dazzling sunlight; the ship seemed to him to be moving more slowly now, and the sea all round them was still empty. They went past what he took to be the ship's main hatch,

120

then down two steps into the bridge accommodation, where the air was noticeably cleaner and cooler.

Outside a cabin door at the far end the young man stopped and turned to Hellier and moistened his lips. He gave a soft mocking chuckle, but said nothing. He knocked on the door and opened it and beckoned Hellier to go in.

It wasn't Ramon, or even Captain Esposito waiting for him there. This was a larger cabin, with two portholes, and some furniture. There were two bunks and on the lower one Esmée lifted an arm and crooked a finger at him. He heard the door close behind him.

'We must have a little talk,' she said sleepily. Her dark hair had been brushed away from her face and tied with a white ribbon; she wore a short white shift with narrow straps that went over her shoulders; nothing else. The electric fan on the bulkhead over her bunk stirred her hair and lifted the front of her shift as she moved to sit up.

'Why not sit down?' she said.

'I'm all right here,' he said.

She laughed and drew her knees up. 'You thought it would be Señor Ramon. Your face is so sour, it is funny.'

'You might be a nice kid if you'd stop trying to act the *femme fatale*.'

'You cannot be in love with that old one

121

back there,' she said. 'That would be too foolish.'

Hellier had moved nearer the bunk. 'Don't you ever think of anything else but the bedroom?'

'Frequently,' she said. 'But I also like to relax myself, it is nature, yes?'

'Listen,' said Hellier, 'one day you'll bump into a man and you'll fall for him like a load of bricks and I hope to hell he beats you, regularly – because you are nothing but an ill-mannered little puss.'

She wriggled on the bunk, and the hem of her shift had slipped into her lap. She giggled with delight, showing him the tip of her tongue.

'You would like to beat me? I know.'

'Just how old are you?' he said. 'You go on like a fifteen year old, and you can pull your skirt down because I'm not in the mood.'

'I have good legs.' She slid them down so that they lay side by side.

'Smashing,' he said. 'I'm swooning with desire.'

She flicked the hem of her skirt down to mid-thigh. 'I do not like men to make fun of me.'

'You can't win them all,' he said cheerfully. 'Write me off as one of your few failures. Let's agree I have other things on my mind, such as what the hell you lot think you are up to.'

'You begin to bore me.'

'Well that was a short lived romance. May I go now?'

'Get me a drink,' she said. 'Whisky, and soda.'

There was a bottle of Scotch and a siphon of soda water on a cabinet at the foot of the bunks, and two glasses. He poured her a modest whisky and soda and brought it over to her. She had been liberal with her perfume, and it drifted over him as she put out her hand to take the glass.

'And yourself,' she said. 'I do not care to drink alone.'

'You make a wonderful hostess, all the right instincts.'

He poured his drink, with plenty of soda. He came round to stand beside her and raised his glass. 'To the speedy severance of our association.'

She stared at her glass, the sharp little teeth nibbling at her lower lip. 'First you bore me, then you offer me an insult.'

He finished his drink in one quick swallow; it was weak enough. 'What did you expect?' he said. 'A Valentine? We're on opposite sides of the fence. We're your prisoners and we don't like it one little bit, so why should I pretend? I'm talking common-sense.'

She was drinking her whisky, sip by sip, thoughtfully, wriggling her toes at herself, and her feet, he then decided, were the least attractive part of her; she had gone too often bare-foot, probably, in her childhood.

'Look,' he said, 'why not let me talk to Ramon, he's your boss, isn't he? Let me talk to him.'

'He will have nothing to tell you. It is not possible.'

'I wish you'd tell me why.'

'Is it not obvious?' She gave him a direct and very searching look. 'We did not wish for your presence, and it is your bad fortune.'

'I seem to have heard that somewhere before,' he said.

'It is the truth. You must accept it.'

'But you're going to put us ashore somewhere, aren't you?' he said. 'You can't ferry us about the Caribbean indefinitely, what in the world is the point of it all? Look at it from our point of view, it's a crazy situation—'

She held out her empty glass. 'Make me another, no soda and make it a real one, I am not a child.'

He sloshed the whisky into the glass and took it over.

'You'll get yourself stoned,' he said. 'Bad for the liver in this climate. You'll lose your looks.'

She drank the whisky as though she had a private grudge against it; he didn't think she really liked it.

'Tell me about Ramon,' he said.

'You have seen him for yourself. Why should I talk about him?'

'He's your boss, he gives the orders, obviously you're all a bit scared of him – what is he after?'

'You should ask him that yourself,' she said. 'And I am far from scared of him, I am scared of nobody.'

'You must have had a beautiful childhood.'

She glared at him, not quite sure how to take it. 'I was brought up properly and with much respect, we are not all savages just because we do not come from your old part of the world, we have our own ideas–'

'And they don't include the liberty of the individual,' he said. 'Such as Mrs Dempster and me. Do you happen to know the penalty in these parts for kidnapping? I know cold-blooded killing doesn't bother any of you, but then, as you say, you have your own ideas. Most civilized people would consider you and Ramon and the rest of your crew just a gang of thugs.'

'You do not have our problems,' she said. 'You are English, yes? We all know your little country is on the way down, there is no spirit in you now, you are bankrupt in everything, you do not count, you are all worn out, the future is with the other peoples, the ones you have been looking down on and despising as your inferiors, and we are not your inferiors. We will make the future for ourselves, we owe you nothing.'

'Very nicely said.' He smiled down at her. 'One small point, why doesn't this ship show any flag? Are you pirates or something like that?'

'Why should we need to wave a coloured piece of rag here on the open ocean?' she said. 'There is nobody to see.'

'It's customary, that's all I meant. I suppose the ship has a name?'

'Naturally. We call her the *Blue Virgin.*' She looked at him and giggled.

'Very apt,' he said.

'And we are not pirates.'

'That's a load off my mind,' he said. 'But you still haven't given me a hint.'

She gave an impatient flick with her free hand. 'You are not important, you and that woman – you found yourself in the wrong place and at the wrong time, it is your misfortune.'

'That's really lovely,' he said. 'So what happens now?'

'You will wait.'

'I'm getting tired of this,' he said.

'You make things more difficult for yourself, and the woman.'

'Her name is Mrs Dempster as you well know.'

Esmée laughed, not at all a nice laugh. 'You have slept with her yet? The stupid Kramer arrived in time to spoil that, did he not? Last night?'

'You must endear yourself to all who meet you,' he said.

She liked that, her eyes screwed themselves up and her bare shoulders lifted. She patted the bunk beside her. 'Give yourself a treat, I will show you what real loving is.'

'I'd sooner bed down with a nest of tarantulas.'

'I could make you change your mind.'

'I doubt it,' he said. 'I'm fussy that way.'

'I have had many lovers, I know what I talk about.'

She had moved herself up so that she sat almost upright with the pillows at her back; she slipped the straps free of her shoulders and let the shift slide down; there was a seriousness in her gesture, a quaint gravity as she looked to him for confirmation that she was beautifully made.

'They do you credit,' he said. 'But if you go on bashing away at all and sundry and lapping up the hard liquor they won't look like that long.'

'There is something wrong with you, perhaps?' she said, and it sounded like a genuine question.

'Nothing at all,' he said. 'I've had no complaints so far, and I'm no monk.'

'You insult me. What is wrong with me?'

He wiped a hand across his face. 'Look, if I hopped into bed with you now, that would be the real insult, to you, because I honestly haven't anything for you, can't you accept that? Making love is too important to waste on a stranger, and that's what I am to you.'

She shook her head slowly, puzzled. 'No man has ever refused me before.'

'I'm sorry,' he said. 'Believe me I am. I would hate an experience as important as that to be just another waste, and you're too beautiful to be satisfied with second best. Don't you agree? I hope that doesn't sound pompous, because I do mean it.'

He gave her the most sincere look he could raise, and he was remembering one or two women who would hoot like hell if they were to hear him so eloquent in refusing such an open invitation.

Esmée thrust out her lower lip, frowning. This was beyond her. She repeated: 'I have not had this before, you are a normal man?'

'I think so,' he said. 'In fact I'm damn sure I am.'

'But you do not desire me?'

'I'd be a liar if I said I didn't,' he told her.

She looked at him under her eyebrows. 'You think I am not good enough for you to make love with. I am no common woman. I choose my lovers, and they do not ever refuse me.'

He groaned and shook his head. 'I wish I could make you understand – I'm paying you a compliment, making love isn't like eating a quick meal, not to me.'

'We have time,' she said. 'Nobody will come.'

'It's the time and the place,' he said. 'They're not right. We're not animals, you're much too beautiful for that – I'll tell you the honest truth, I've never seen a more lovely girl, I don't know anything else about you, but you are beautiful. You don't need me.' He could feel the sweat trickling down his armpits, and it wasn't altogether from the heat in the cabin.

She slipped the straps of her shift up over her shoulders. 'If you ever talk of this,' she said softly, 'I will have you killed.'

'I'd be too ashamed, I haven't anything to boast about. And nobody would ever believe me, not if they'd seen you.'

She nodded. 'I will tell you something – you would not wish me to send Didi to your woman, you have met Didi, he brought you to me – it was in my mind to send him to her for the afternoon. He is a famous lover, very strong. He is very bad for a woman like her – she would not be happy.'

He waited for a moment, and she fussed needlessly with the pillows at her back. It was a tricky stage, and he had no reason to doubt that she could do just what she had said, if she chose. Didi the stallion. Bad for a woman like Eileen. He felt a cold knot tighten in the pit of his stomach, and he shoved his hands into the pockets of his slacks so that she shouldn't notice what he wanted to do with them then and there.

'A woman as attractive as you are wouldn't do a thing like that,' he said. 'It wouldn't be natural. She hasn't been a widow very long.'

'She is nothing to me.'

'You might find yourself sorry for her in the end. You have all your life in front of you.'

'I could get to like you,' she said reflectively, 'if it were possible, you are not altogether a fool, I think.'

He smiled at her. 'All right if I leave now?'

She said nothing so he walked to the door, and he was expecting her to call him back. She didn't. And when he looked back from the open door she was staring up at the roof of the cabin, her arms straight by her sides, palms uppermost. He nearly began to feel sorry for her. With her one-track mind she was surely heading for a lot of grief.

Before climbing up on deck he wiped his streaming face. He half expected to find Didi waiting to escort him back, but there was nobody about. Nobody was ever going to believe his version of what almost happened back there in her scented cabin. The sunlight up on deck was blinding, and

130

the ship had hardly any way at all.

When he paused at the rail to look down at the quiet oily water slowly sliding past he knew he was under observation from the bridge, and he met the knowing grin from the officer on watch and shook his head and gave a doleful thumbs-down. Man to man, the officer shifted one shoulder in sympathy. Probably every sailor on board knew where he had been and why. Didi would surely be a blabber-mouth.

He went below and found Eileen sitting on her bunk, and at her expectant smile he shrugged, and said: 'I didn't get any information, I'm afraid. It wasn't Ramon. It was the girl, Esmée. She wouldn't tell me anything. I tried. Sorry.'

'What did she want then?'

'She was bored,' he said lightly. 'She thought I might provide some diversion. I had to disappoint her.'

'How very awkward for you.' Her smile was friendly and her voice understanding, just faintly amused.

'I was the perfect little gent. She wasn't being too subtle.'

'That I can imagine. I began to wonder what was happening.'

'Nothing,' he said. 'Except some fast talk from me, but I preserved my virtue intact.'

She laughed softly. 'It's been a long afternoon. We're not going very fast, are we?'

'Nearly stopped,' he agreed. 'In mid-ocean. Nothing else in sight that I could see. I couldn't even find out where we're supposed to be going, but wherever it is they don't seem to be in any hurry now. They whipped us off the island in a hell of a rush at dawn, that must have been in case there was any search starting. I haven't noticed any aircraft about, have you?'

'It's too early,' she said. 'And now we're miles away. They'll never come looking for us on this little boat. You must be regretting you ever met my husband, you wouldn't be here otherwise.'

'No point in thinking like that,' he said. 'We're both here – and I'm not writing us off.'

'We can't do anything, you know we can't, James. You don't have to pretend for my benefit.'

He took one of her hands in both of his. 'Now hear this,' he said. 'We're not pretending. Just waiting. I don't know what for – but something will happen, you see.'

'I don't see anything,' she said.

Chapter Ten

She had been lying on her bunk for a long time, still and very quiet, although he knew she wasn't sleeping. It was as though she had chosen to withdraw from him and her unhappy surroundings; he had been quite unable to persuade her that there could be anything in front of them but disaster.

'I wish I had some clean clothes,' she burst out suddenly. 'I hate being so squalid ... on top of all the rest, it's too vile!'

'It's rough,' he agreed, surprised at her violence. 'I bet she has plenty of spare gear, Esmée. Would you like me to try? I think I've softened her a little–'

'No thank you. I'd rather remain as I am.'

'You look fine to me,' he said.

'I'm sorry,' she said, turning her head on the bolster to face him. 'Don't mind me.'

'I mind you very much,' he said. 'And I think you're pretty good all round.'

'That girl Esmée,' she said, 'didn't she tell you anything?'

'Nothing that we don't know already. They didn't expect to find us on the island – we've got in the way of some stunt or other, I can't even guess what it is, but they didn't want us around then.'

'That much is obvious from the way they've been treating us,' she said.

'Esmée gave me a pep talk on racial discrimination in the past, us and them – effete European whites, the usual line – what would you say she is? Some kind of a half-caste?'

'Part Spanish a long way back, I should imagine. Creole. Most of the islanders have mixed blood ... the women are often very beautiful when they're young, she is.'

'Fierce and too forthright for my taste,' he said.

'I've been remembering something,' she said. 'Not many years ago, those Portuguese rebels or insurgents or whatever they were, didn't they capture a pleasure cruiser? It was somewhere in the Caribbean – you must remember it, it made all the head-lines–'

'I remember it,' he said. 'They came aboard as passengers and hi-jacked the ship when she was at sea – very smooth job, as I recall it. A load of passengers on board, most of them thrilled to bits. Piracy up to date. A demonstration against the Salazar regime. Right? What brings that up?'

'That was a really big ship,' she said. 'A modern liner on a sunshine cruise, it wasn't like this little thing, was it?'

'Not much, what's the point?'

'For some days nobody knew where the liner was, they completely lost it, didn't they? A big ship like that, and they had everything out looking for it, planes and warships, and they couldn't find it, so what chance is there for us in this little thing? Nobody is going to notice it.'

'Maybe not,' he said.

'Well then?'

'They'll have to put in somewhere, they can't cart us around indefinitely. That'll be our chance. So we sit tight until then.'

'Couldn't we bargain with them?' she said.

'You mean offer them money?'

'Yes, if we're such a nuisance to them they ought to be glad to get us off their hands.'

He held out one empty palm, blew on it and shut his fingers and grinned. 'They'd be insulted at what I could offer. I don't even have a job any more.'

'I could raise funds,' she said. 'I'm a widow. I could find a lot of money if they gave us time.'

He rubbed the side of his nose. 'I haven't any claim on you.'

'Don't be silly,' she said. 'It's for both of us. I wouldn't try it without you – you don't imagine I'd try to buy myself free and leave you with them, do you?'

'All right,' he said and smiled. 'We'll try to make a package deal, but I don't feel too optimistic.'

'What have we got to lose?' she said.

'Only money,' he said cheerfully. 'Your money. I don't think for one minute that we'll have any luck with Ramon or Esmée, or even Captain Esposito, I can't see them letting us free for money – quite apart from the murder of your husband and Ahen Toong, we've been kidnapped and that's no laughing matter in any court.'

She slid her legs over the side of the bunk and stood up and did the best she could with her creased clothes, tidying her hair. There was suddenly a purposeful air about her.

'You don't think it'll work,' she said.

'Dicey. Where are you off to?'

'I'm going to chat up some of the crew, find out where we're going.' She slipped neatly past him and out into the companionway. 'I still have the freedom of the deck, you haven't. They won't mind me wandering about.'

She emerged into the sunlight and sauntered idly over to the rail to look down at the water, just like any passenger killing time at sea; there were two men on the bridge and one of them had a kind of a nautical cap with a peak and some braid; a muscular negro was squatting beside a piece of machinery in the stern, working on it with a large spanner; he wore a baseball cap and a pair of khaki shorts and his torso shone; he had seen her appear on deck, he had given her a grin and now he was back at work, humming to himself.

She couldn't approach him while those two on the bridge were watching. She didn't hurry. There was a radio playing up for'ard, and now and then she could hear men's voices. What size crew would they need to run a boat like this? A dozen? She had brought their cigarette supply with her – smoking helped her to feel at leisure, she thought.

After a while she sat on the hatch cover and went through the pretence of sunbathing, leaning back on her elbows. Twice she changed position until she was now close under the bridge, and the man with the cap had come across so that he was gazing straight down on her, and there was nothing in his attitude to suggest he was about to order her below.

The braided cap was pushed to the back of his head; he had a long brown face with a wide mouth; his shirt was open at the neck and it was whiter than white; he had put a cigar into his mouth but hadn't lit it.

She caught his eye and she fancied he was about to smile, so she smiled first and ducked her head in greeting; he removed the cigar and gave it a short wave, and now his smile was friendly enough.

'Are you the captain?' she said.

'*Si,* Señorita – Fernando Murphy.'

'How do you do,' she said. 'I'm Mrs Dempster.'

'Escuse, Señora.'

'I like your ship,' she said.

Captain Fernando Murphy wagged his head from side to side deprecatingly. 'She is little, but she goes well.'

Eileen was standing at the foot of a steep little ladder that led up to the bridge. 'I've never seen how you steer a ship, it must be very difficult. Would it be all right if I came up just for a little peep, Captain?'

'My pleasure, Señora. I will show you–'

Her legs were trembling as they climbed the steel rungs of the ladder; he gave her a hand up the last few, and then she realized what a little man he was. Shorter than herself, even with that captain's cap on; he needed a shave and his breath had the sickly sweet heaviness of rum.

Through a glass panel she could see the man at the helm, the rows of instruments in front of him; he seemed very young; he took one quick glance at her and then went back to his steering, and she thought he was scared at the Captain's presence.

'Now I will show you how we are finding our way in all these waters, Señora,' said Fernando Murphy, preparing to take her into the wheelhouse.

'Please, Captain,' she said, 'it's so nice out

here, I love the view up here.'

He followed her to the far corner of the flying bridge, and together they leaned on the rail and watched the bows slide along; there was just a little swell, a soothing rocking up and down, and a stir of breeze.

'Where are we going, Captain?' she said.

'Señora, I regret, it is not permitted, I am desolated to refuse the Señora–'

She smiled at him and nudged his elbow on the rail. 'Don't tell me you're scared of Ramon, not a man like you, I don't believe it, Captain.'

'It is a business contract, a man must live, Señora.' He had straightened up and she thought he was going to escort her off the bridge.

She touched his arm. 'Please listen to me.'

He turned his back to the breeze and took out his matches, then lit his cigar, darting shrewd little glances at her as he puffed. He flicked the spent match over the rail.

'Señora,' he said quietly, 'I am a man with responsibilities – I am not able to please myself.'

'Five thousand dollars,' she said, 'If you will help me and my friend to get off your ship safely.'

He looked at the end of his cigar. 'You have no money with you–'

'But I can get it,' she broke in eagerly, 'there won't be any difficulty. As soon as we're free I can arrange to have it credited to any bank you name–'

'And when I go to the bank to collect the money – there will be the police.'

'No, no,' she said, 'it won't be like that, I promise you, the police will have nothing to do with it.'

'You are in bad trouble, Señora. So you will promise anything.'

'This will be between you and me,' she said earnestly. 'I can get the money.'

'Talk is cheap,' said Fernando Murphy.

'I'm telling you the truth,' she insisted.

'You do not know how much you ask,' he said. 'This is not your part of the world, and you do not understand how things are done with us – it is not so simple as you think, Señora.'

'You can do it,' she went on in a quieter tone. 'You can arrange to get us off your ship, tonight … lend us a rowing boat when we're passing near one of the islands, something like that, when it's dark…'

Now his gaze was fixed for'ard, he was pulling hard at his cigar, his hands clasped behind his back, the regulation stance of the Captain on his bridge.

'If you prefer to have cash,' she said, 'that'll be all right, I can have it ready for you to pick up any place you choose.'

'You do not understand the difficulties, Señora,' he said. 'Señor Ramon would not be deceived – he has been a very good friend to me. We have been doing good business together, and he pays well.'

'Twenty thousand,' said Eileen. 'Isn't that enough?'

'Señor Ramon would make things very unpleasant, he is a man of much power.'

'I am very glad to hear you admit it, Fernando,' said a quiet voice behind them.

Eileen turned, her back against the rail. Ramon still wore the crumpled suit, and the yellowing straw hat was in his hand. 'The lady should not be here, Fernando. The bridge is forbidden to all passengers–'

'Passengers!' said Eileen violently. 'You mean prisoners, don't you?'

'Now you are being quite unreasonable,' said Ramon in a mildly reproving tone. 'You must not interrupt the Captain in the discharging of his duties.'

'It was a little friendly talk,' said Fernando Murphy. 'There has been no harm done.'

'I am sure of it,' said Ramon. 'Twenty thousand, Fernando? For doing what?'

'It was nothing, Señor Ramon, I do assure you. I was letting her talk, and now I am thinking she is a crazy woman.'

Eileen glared with contempt at Fernando. Perhaps he was being clever, hoping to put Ramon off; but she thought it more likely that he was just plain scared of Ramon.

'I'm crazy all right,' she said angrily. 'I

141

thought you might have some guts.'

Fernando avoided her eye. Ramon looked down over the rail and beckoned to someone out of sight. 'Come and remove her,' he said.

'I'm staying right here,' said Eileen. 'I've had enough of jumping around at your whim–'

Didi's head appeared at the top of the ladder, then his naked torso and the rest of him in the blue slacks. The rings glinted on his fingers as he swung himself up and slapped both bare feet on the deck; that full red mouth was wide and grinning, and a tight curl of black hair bounced on his forehead as he danced over to where Eileen waited, flipping his long fingers in her face.

'You lay a hand on me,' she said, 'and I'll maim you... I'll ruin you–'

Didi lifted his shoulders in delight, poking out his tongue at her, chuckling, swinging his hips from side to side as though they were about to be partners in some frenzied dance.

'Get away from me!' The rail was at her back.

Didi pouted his lips at her, ducked to one side, then darted at her and took her round the waist before she could jab her knee up into his groin. He had pulled her violently into his embrace, arching himself against her so that she had to let go of the rail to hit at his grinning face – and even that was a failure, because he turned her and swung her over his shoulder, one arm clamped across her thighs, her head hanging down behind him. It couldn't have been more ignominious. When she tried to kick her legs he gave her a resounding slap and she heard the laughter.

He was carrying her down the ladder, and she dared not struggle because if he let her go she would fall straight down on her head; she could smell the rank maleness of his body, and when her face brushed against the working muscles of his back she felt sick and more frightened than ever; he was alive with triumph, and the hand that pinned her thighs was exploring and spreading over her.

He jumped the last few rungs of the ladder and the jolt knocked all the breath out of her and her hair fell over her face. But they had a new audience, she could tell that without having to look. He was parading her along the deck now, shuffling and slapping his feet, crooning over her arched body.

With a wild triumphant shout he began to whirl her around and around; her head swam and she could hear herself screaming against his voice and the shouts of the onlookers, and she knew that if it went on much longer she would probably faint. When suddenly he became still she felt too weak to do anything at first but get her breath, and when she was able to see again there just below her head was the handle of his knife in its leather sheath, snug behind his right hip.

She got her fingers around the handle and tugged and the knife came free, but before she could do any more she felt herself tossed in the air, over his shoulder. She landed heavily on the deck and slid against the edge of the hatch cover, and the knife was in her hand.

Didi had his back to her, and through his straddled legs she saw James Hellier. He wasn't looking at her, and there was an expression on his face unlike any she had ever seen before, and it made her catch her breath with its very intentness.

Didi settled himself, laughing softly. 'Gonna carve you good, *compadre*–'

Hellier came on very steadily, seeing nothing but Didi's shining face. From the bridge Ramon shouted but nobody took any notice. A fight was a fight, and Didi was known to be spectacular with a knife. Esmée had now appeared, in a white robe, and the crew made room for her in front of the bridge accommodation.

His mouth wide open in pleasurable anticipation, Didi felt behind him for the knife and his fingers found the empty sheath, and his mouth fell open wider still, and he darted an anxious look around to see what room he had to retreat.

Hellier had been expecting a knife, and he had given himself one immediate objective – he was going to break that arm and take that knife. Somehow. No knife. Just the two of them. Good. The crowd would be rooting for Didi. All right. Just let them stay there and watch. Fate owed him that much surely. He had been generating a lot of steam.

He feinted at Didi's belly, brought his hands down, and clipped him across the jaw. It was too easy. He did it again, and again it worked, harder this time, and Didi's pretty mouth was bleeding. Nobody was going to interfere.

Ramon on the bridge was waving his arms. Esmée smiled; she loved watching men fight, really fight, preferably with knives, but this was amusing enough; it would do Didi no harm to have a beating in front of the others.

Eileen had dragged herself out of the way, the knife in her hand. When she got to her feet the harsh sunlight picked out the two struggling men, and she caught the expression on Esmée's face – James had backed Didi up against the rail and he was hitting him methodically and viciously in the face, and Didi was grunting as his head was shifted from side to side.

It couldn't go on. Didi slipped to one

knee. Hellier stopped punching. The audience began to jeer at the tame ending. Didi launched himself forward, thrusting himself off with the flat of his kneeling foot, his head caught Hellier below the belt and Didi's arms wrapped themselves around his thighs, and as Hellier hit the deck Didi began to claw his way up, reaching for Hellier's throat.

He got one hand over Hellier's windpipe, but the other missed and Hellier bit it hard as it slipped over his mouth. He wrapped both hands deep in Didi's thick hair and shoved with all his strength, and felt the pressure on his own throat lessen, but the hair was oily and he couldn't hold his grip, and Didi still had the upper berth, for a while – but his mouth was a mess, so Hellier added to the damage with his elbow, there wasn't too much force in it, but it was enough to have Didi easing off.

They rolled over, side by side, and Didi was making animal noises that frothed the blood from his broken mouth. Without his knife Didi was only half a fighter, but he wasn't done with yet. Like the strike of a cobra, he jack-knifed both legs and kicked Hellier in the groin, and he was so quick that there was no time for Hellier to tuck himself away, and those bare feet had been hardened and toughened, and Hellier had to coil down over himself in agony.

Shaking his head, dribbling blood over the deck, Didi crawled free, whimpering. He had immediate flight in mind, then his sight cleared and he saw the woman there by the rail, with his knife in her hand – his knife. *Aiye.* He pulled himself upright, and lunged at her. She held her hand out over the rail, and as he grabbed her arm she opened her fingers, and there was nothing he could do as the knife fell, the blade glinting briefly as it dropped out of sight.

Shaking with frustration, he lifted his fist – he would throw the bitch into the sea as well. Then his head was jerked back with such violence that he was sure his neck would snap. Hellier's forearm closed about his windpipe from behind, he was being forced to his knees, and now there was a frightening weight pressing into the small of his back, his whole spine was being forced out into an arc, and the pain was beyond endurance.

His back would break and death would come, soon … *Mother of God* … there was a surging in his ears. The face of the woman was dancing in front of him, and he could say nothing to her; his frenzied eyes had to plead for him before the darkness enveloped him.

The audience had fallen very still, so that they all heard Eileen's breathless: 'No–'

Hellier lifted his knee from Didi's back, let

him fall to the deck, and took a deep quavering breath – only Didi would know how near he had been to sudden death. Hellier lifted his hand and Eileen came over to him and they went together along the deck without looking back.

Esmée shoved her way through the crowd before Ramon could get down from the bridge. Didi hadn't moved, only his shoulders shook, and they seemed to have lost some of their muscular splendour. Contemptuously Esmée turned the body over, using her foot, and Didi hid his face and sobbed.

'Take him below,' Ramon snapped. 'Clean him up–'

Esmée's face was ugly as she said: 'Why bother? He is trash.' Esmée had no time for losers among her men, and Didi had served his turn.

She was looking at Ramon as Didi was hauled below. 'We could have a use for that one,' she said. 'You should hire him, uncle.'

Chapter Eleven

Ramon made an impatient gesture and turned to look at the sea; they had the deck to themselves; on his bridge Fernando Murphy was making little effort to hide his satisfaction at the outcome of the recent conflict – he had no liking for Didi.

'You know nothing of men beyond the ability to please you in the bed,' said Ramon. 'You are young, you can see little beyond your own body.'

'So?' said Esmée softly. 'I am a woman.'

'This Hellier,' said Ramon, 'we could do nothing with him; he fights well but only when it is in his own interest. I have met his kind of man before. He is a solitary one. He will do what he chooses to do – we could not depend on him.'

'The woman,' said Esmée. 'We might get at him through the woman – he was ready to kill Didi because he saw him handling the woman; we need a man like Hellier – or we should kill him quickly. It must be one thing or the other, uncle.'

'You sent for him this afternoon,' said Ramon. 'That was against my orders.'

She linked her arm in his. 'It was nothing,

I was bored.'

'I have very little patience with you when you are in this mood, we have important things in front of us, and they will demand all our efforts–'

'Uncle,' she interrupted gently, 'I need no sermon from you, when the time arrives I will not be the last to move, you know that – have you ever seen me frightened?'

He patted her hand where it rested on his arm. 'You are my brother's daughter. We have nothing to do with fear.'

'So you will not try to make use of Hellier?' she said.

'I have yet to decide,' said Ramon stiffly. 'We have not had good experience in using outsiders–'

'Hellier is not Kramer,' she said. She freed her arm and went below, confident that she had said just enough to have Ramon doubting his own plans, and Uncle Ramon was a great one for planning and for trying to cover all contingencies; improvisation made him uneasy – and all of their planning had been based on the assumption that Dempster and his servant would be the only ones on the island.

The unexpected presence of Mrs Dempster and Hellier had forced Ramon to change his plans, and he never liked that; it diminished his leadership, and Ramon was always very strong on leadership.

Ramon let an hour pass before he sent Captain Esposito to bring Hellier to the saloon; the day was fading, and the sunlight slashed through the portholes, showing up the cracked leather padding of the chairs and the scarred table top. Ramon sat alone, his jacket off and his sleeves rolled up; there was an unlabelled bottle and two glasses on the table. He motioned Hellier to sit, and Esposito withdrew.

Ramon pushed over the bottle and a glass. 'If you know rum, Señor, you will find this a pleasant experience.'

Hellier poured a drink and shoved the bottle back. 'It'll take more than a bottle of rum to make any of this pleasant to me.'

Ramon gave himself a drink. 'You are a violent man,' he said.

'What do you expect?' said Hellier. 'You ought to keep your thugs under better control.'

'I applaud your chivalry,' said Ramon, his face stiff.

'You can stuff it,' said Hellier.

'But I am serious, Señor.' Ramon had spread long bony forearms over the table. 'I regret the necessity of what has been happening to you, and Mrs Dempster.'

'Whatever you're short of it isn't gall,' said Hellier. 'Who the hell do you think you are?' He slapped the table and the bottle danced along with the glasses. 'Why don't you fly a flag like any law-abiding craft? Or is that another state secret?'

'Señor,' said Ramon, 'there are many things to explain–'

'And you'd better make it good,' said Hellier sourly.

'You find yourself in a position of some difficulty,' said Ramon, 'and you must believe that I fully understand your feelings, it has all been most unfortunate.'

'I could put it another way,' said Hellier.

Ramon folded his long fingers together. 'I have thought of making you an offer.'

'You must be out of your mind,' said Hellier. 'What kind of an offer?'

'You are evidently a man of decision and some integrity. I am engaged on a project of considerable delicacy. There is admittedly an element of risk – I think you might be interested, Señor. I might have room for you.'

'Delicacy?' said Hellier. 'We don't speak the same language, there's nothing delicate about you – I don't like your light-hearted view of human life.'

'It would pay well.'

'If I lived to collect. What's the project?'

'Then you would be interested?'

'You're jumping ahead of yourself – I'm thinking of a trigger-happy character named Kramer and what happened to him when he stopped being useful to you and your gang

152

of assassins, he was a plain honest-to-God killer, I'm not–'

'That much is clear,' agreed Ramon.

'If I have to make a guess,' said Hellier, 'I'd say you must be gun-running, or something similar, I expect there's money at the end of it somewhere, there always is, hence all the cloak and dagger nonsense.'

'You take a low view of human nature,' said Ramon.

Hellier laughed. 'Coming from you that's good.'

'There are other things of value beyond money, Señor.' Ramon's face was long and solemn.

'Personal freedom?' said Hellier. 'But you wouldn't know anything about that, would you? You just stick a gun into people and that settles the argument, you've been living in the trees too long.'

'You talk too much but say little, Señor. Freedom comes in many guises, and for many of us it has to be fought for, if it is to be of any value.'

'Then you can make a start with this bit,' said Hellier. 'If you want me to listen to you there's one thing you have to do – you liberate Mrs Dempster and me from this ship, anything less than that is just hot air and I'm not interested.'

'You should think it over,' said Ramon placidly, as though he had not expected any other reply. 'It is not an offer I may have the time to repeat.'

'You haven't made an offer,' said Hellier. 'I want some details.'

'In general terms,' said Ramon. 'I cannot be more precise at this stage.'

'You're being too coy.' Hellier shunting his glass of rum from one hand to the other, sliding it over the table, watching the dark liquid tilt; it was truly excellent rum.

'Here's an idea,' said Hellier. 'You arrange to put Mrs Dempster ashore somewhere where she can get back to civilisation, and as soon as I know that's been done, you and I will confer, how's that?'

'It would not be possible,' said Ramon. 'She would talk and my business is too important to be endangered by a woman talking.'

'It must be one hell of a business if you expect Mrs Dempster to forget her murdered husband and his servant, and then all the rest of it ... you must be inhabiting a fantasy world all of your own.'

'Señor,' said Ramon stiffly, 'I doubt if you will ever meet a saner man than myself – I know what I am about.'

'There was an Irishman once,' said Hellier, 'and he was sure he was the only bloke in step in the regiment. Thanks for the drink, I'll find my own way back to the cells.'

He got up and left. Ramon called after

him softly, but he kept on going. As a conference it had been doomed right from the start – Ramon couldn't seriously have thought he might join him in whatever he was on? Not after what he had seen?

Pausing along midway past the main hatch he thought of his suggestion – gun-running was still a highly profitable business in the area, but who might be the customers? Perhaps it hadn't been such a wild surmise after all, although there had been no reaction from Ramon. A small revolution brewing somewhere nearby? That wouldn't be any novelty. With the island used as a staging-post, maybe? It might begin to make sense that way.

Eileen was waiting in her cabin. He shook his head. 'Negative,' he said. 'It was the old buzzard himself, Ramon. He didn't tell me a thing. There was a round-about suggestion that I might consider joining him in whatever racket he's in. I don't really believe he meant it, but he said he did. He was very cagey all through. Absolutely no details. Just vague talk. So finally I upped and left.'

'You'd almost think they're playing some kind of a game with us,' she said.

'I think we may have bumped into one end of a gun-running outfit. I put it to Ramon but he ignored it, naturally.'

'I've had the same idea,' she said. 'I've

been remembering something Edward said years ago. He'd been approached by some group of political operators, I don't remember the exact details because we didn't talk business, not usually, but I do recall this instance because he sounded so very emphatic about it – it was an arms shipment of some sort, and he wouldn't have anything to do with it. That was long before he had the island. I believe lots of people with trading contacts made money out of illegal arms deals, and I suppose they still do, but I'm sure Edward wasn't in it ever. He didn't need to be, he was making plenty of money legitimately.'

'I'm only guessing,' said Hellier. 'There are always political explosions boiling up here and there, and they all need hardware.'

'I wish I'd been a bit smarter when I tried to bribe the captain,' she said. 'I think he was weakening. Fernando Murphy.' She smiled. 'How do you suppose he came by a name like that?'

'It's a long way from old county Cork,' said Hellier. 'But those Irish sailors were great travellers in their time. How much did you offer him?'

'I opened at five thousand dollars,' she said.

'Very handsome – two and a half thousand each. A bargain, I'd say.'

'I really did think I had him dangling,' she

said. 'My final bid was twenty thousand, and I thought he was going to bite – then Ramon came and spoilt it.'

'Pity,' said Hellier.

'I think Ramon overheard what I was trying to do. I don't know how long he was there behind us on the bridge.'

'Twenty thousand,' said Hellier thoughtfully. 'We just might hear more from Fernando.'

'I don't think so,' she said. 'He seemed terribly scared of Ramon.'

'They all are,' said Hellier. 'Except us.' He smiled at her. 'Am I right?'

'I don't know,' she said. 'I've gone beyond being frightened. I'm not being brave, far from it... I'm just numbed, I don't seem able to feel anything much. I'm all muddled and bewildered – if I thought it might do me any good I'd probably start weeping again, but I don't suppose I can even do that any more. I've never come across murder and violence and all this senseless fighting, not at first hand–'

'Few people do,' he said. 'The lucky ones.'

'I'm hating it, all of it,' she said passionately.

Night came down very suddenly, after a torrid sunset, and it was evident that the *Blue Virgin* was making much better progress; it was no longer a leisurely cruise in the sunlight, and the whole ship was shaking with the pounding of the engines. Nobody came near them, not even to bring supper, and for a long time they both sat on the top step of the companionway to get the air. There was a blue-black sky and a dark sea and no stars yet. In the shaded light from the bridge they could see the heads of the men on duty, moving about. All the sea was still theirs.

The evening hours crawled by, and Hellier was quite sure now that they would be making a landfall somewhere in the course of the night; something was going to happen; they had been ambling along all through the day, now they were hurrying and still showing no lights.

'I hope Fernando Murphy knows his business, belting along at this rate, it wouldn't help us much if he ran us aground. How are we fixed for cigarettes?' said Hellier.

Eileen took out the packet. 'One each,' she said.

Later on supper arrived, unsweetened black coffee and some dry biscuits, on a tin tray, brought by a large silent sailor with the biggest hands Hellier had ever seen; a zombie of a man. Hellier gave him a good evening and some earthy comments about the poorness of the fare, and the sailor didn't even look at him, he just dumped the tray outside Eileen's door and stalked off.

'The service is not what it was,' said Hellier. 'Remind me to complain to Ramon when I see him next.'

'James,' she said, a mug of coffee halfway to her lips, 'what do you think is going to happen? To us, I mean?'

'We're slowing down,' he said. 'Listen...'

The *Blue Virgin's* vibrations had lessened; they heard the clanging of the engine room bell, repetitive and sharp. Carrying part of his meagre supper with him, Hellier took a quick look out and saw just the dark outline of what he knew must be land, it didn't move and it showed no lights, so they had arrived somewhere; there were men on the deck up for'ard, and on the bridge.

The *Blue Virgin* slipped placidly on, the water slapping at her sides; it was impossible to guess in that light just how far off the land was or how big it was – a secret rendezvous in the middle of the Caribbean.

Eileen was kneeling beside him and he could feel how her breathing had quickened; she would know as well as he did that they might expect something unpleasant to be happening to them very soon.

They heard the harsh rattling of the anchor chain, then they could see Fernando Murphy and Ramon on the end of the flying bridge, looking out over the water towards the land, and from the bridge a torch flickered on and off rapidly. Ten minutes later they heard the splashing of oars and the creaking of rowlocks, and a boat with two men sidled up and came alongside.

There was some confused shouting, the rope ladder was lowered and one man presently pulled himself aboard and went aloft into the bridge; he went into a huddle with Ramon and Fernando Murphy, and there was some arm-waving.

'I'd give both ears to hear what they're saying,' Hellier whispered. 'They look friendly enough... I wonder where we are? We're only a couple of hundred yards out – do you think we could swim for it? Drop over the side and take a chance?'

She shook her head. 'I don't think I could manage it, not in the dark – do you think we should?'

'Better than staying here, there must be a town of some sort...'

'There aren't any lights anywhere,' she said. 'But if you really think it's the best thing–'

They saw a sailor cross the deck with a bulky package in his arms; he called down to the man out of sight in the boat, and then began to lower the package on the end of a rope. The man in the boat appeared and climbed aboard, slapped the other on the shoulder, laughed and went for'ard.

Moving stiffly and with much caution,

Ramon came down from the bridge. As he turned to go below he saw Hellier's head. He shouted something and waved an arm and it was not in greeting.

'Damn,' said Hellier softly, squatting now too late in the shelter of the companionway. Sharp voices sounded from under the bridge accommodation, and it was no surprise when Captain Esposito arrived, trotting importantly aft.

'You will now be locked in your cabins,' he announced in an outraged voice and with a peremptory gesture. 'This is an order.'

'Both of us?' said Hellier. 'Is that quite necessary?'

'It is an order. Now!'

'Lock us up together,' said Hellier, grinning. 'I'm feeling too nervous to be alone.'

'Do not attempt to make a fool of me,' said Esposito.

'You can't make an order out of that,' said Hellier.

'Hurry!' Esposito pushed him in the back. 'You will both now go to your cabins!' He pushed Hellier in the back again, much harder.

Hellier had been moving off obediently. Now he halted, swung on his heel, his left fist crooked in a tight hook. It was the luckiest punch he would ever throw, and the best timed; it had behind it all the pent-up venom and frustration of the last twenty-four hours.

Esposito walked right on to it. His eyes rolled up, and he fell as stiff as a stick, and his head rapped sickeningly on the steel plates.

'I didn't mean to do that ... it just came on...' Hellier sucked his knuckles. 'Now we'll really have to leave–'

He dragged Esposito into his cabin, went through his pockets, found a handkerchief and shoved it into his mouth. Then he took the revolver from Esposito's holster, turned him over on his face and shoved him under the bunk, it was a tight fit and so much the better. He had taken the keys from Esposito's pocket and one of them fitted the cabin. Then he grabbed Eileen's hand and dragged her along to the companionway.

There was a sailor on guard on deck, just by the ladder, leaning on the rail, smoking, his back half-turned to them; evidently he hadn't heard anything of Esposito's disaster.

'Now listen,' Hellier whispered. 'I'll fix that one up there – you come up right after me and get down the ladder to the boat – never mind what's happening, just get down the ladder – you got that?'

She nodded, her eyes wide and dark. He tapped her cheek with one finger. 'Right after me,' he whispered. 'Don't wait for anything else–'

He clubbed Esposito's gun, crept to the top step, waited a moment. There was somebody on the bridge, but not looking their way; there was plenty of talking going on up for'ard.

Hellier darted across the deck. The sailor by the rail shifted his position, now presenting his back, he was about to move away; he had just tossed his cigarette over the side and he cleared his throat noisily.

Hellier reached him, lifted the gun and swung it hard against the sailor's temple. Just once was enough, and there was no sound as the body slumped and Hellier caught it in his free hand and eased it to the deck.

Eileen was right on cue. She ducked under the rail to get at the ladder, and twelve feet below the boat bobbed against the *Blue Virgin's* plates where the dark water gurgled.

Chapter Twelve

They went down that swaying rope ladder so close together that Hellier trod on her fingers and they landed in a tangled heap in the bottom of the boat, and he had to crawl over her to cast off. There were two stubby oars, but first of all he began to manhandle the boat along so as to pass under the ship's stern and so to the open side, away from the island.

He guessed they only had minutes to spare at the most, and the obvious area for a search would be between the ship and the shore, so they would go the other way, for a start.

They had just got clear of the stern when the shouting began, some very angry shouting, and Hellier began to pull out into the sheltering darkness, because now every yard was going to be precious.

Just four or five uninterrupted minutes, Hellier was praying for no more than that – just long enough to get them well clear of the reflected light from the *Blue Virgin*. There mustn't be anything to direct attention their way. Not yet. Please not yet – they deserved that much luck. Huddled in the stern, Eileen was saying nothing.

There were plenty of lights coming on now; men were crowding the rail where the ladder dangled; somebody on the bridge had found a powerful torch and its wide beam was swinging over the water, backwards and forwards. And all the while Hellier pulled and pulled and hoped, and most of the time he didn't dare look at the ship in case that torch had been transferred to their side. If it began to quarter their area of sea that would be the end – it was taking him a hell of a long time to put any real distance between them and the ship.

When he was forced to snatch a short rest he noticed the drift of the boat and realized that he had been trying to row across the current, so he turned them and let the current help, and the difference in their pace was appreciable. As far as he could judge in the darkness their course now ran roughly parallel to where the *Blue Virgin* lay. That was all right, he hoped, so long as he didn't lose contact with that island there. He put in twenty fast strokes and they bubbled smartly along, and without too much splashing.

He couldn't keep it up too long, and when he eased off he said. 'I think we've nearly done it – thank the Lord for a nice dark night. How do you feel now?'

'All right,' she said and her voice was shaky. 'Never a dull moment.'

'They seem to be lowering a boat,' he said. 'If they'd done it five minutes earlier they might have spotted us ... so long as they think we've made for the nearest beach we'll have a sporting chance. I can't see their boat – I hope that means they can't see us...'

He put in another burst of twenty, this time it finished a little untidily.

Resuming at a more sober pace, he said: 'I wish I knew just where we are, I don't want to head out into the open sea, and there seems to be one hell of a current running across here. Come to think of it, I was never too handy with a pair of oars – it was never my favourite way of working up a lather.'

There was the sound of a shot away in the darkness, and another, then some faint shouting; the beam of the torch from the ship lit up a rowing boat which appeared to carry too many oarsmen. The light jiggled about and then shifted around, turning in their direction but the beam now fell far too short, although Hellier momentarily shipped his oars and waited – there just might be somebody on the bridge with a pair of night glasses who just might pick up the movement of the oars. The light shifted off and went out.

A few minutes later there was a quick burst of what was clearly automatic fire; it was repeated twice more. 'I'm afraid Captain Esposito will find himself reduced to the ranks over this,' said Hellier. 'They're spraying all that hardware over the beach regardless.'

'That was a terrible punch you gave him,' said Eileen.

'A lucky one,' he said, 'and we needed it. What was in that package they dropped?'

It was a small sack, and the rope was still tied to it. Eileen undid the rope and rummaged about and there was a chinking sound; she drew out a bottle of milk, and then another, then two loaves of bread and a large segment of cheese, wrapped in foil.

'Odd,' said Hellier. 'Basic rations – nothing else?'

She spread out the empty sack to show him, then put the items of food back in. 'They'll be very welcome,' she said. 'But I don't understand why they're here. Shift over, I'm coming up there, I can pull on an oar for a bit.'

Side by side they eventually managed to work up a fair rhythm, not fast but steady, and the lights of the *Blue Virgin* now were a healthy distance away. They could just make out the dark outlines of the land to their right, and Hellier's idea was to row as far along as they could before attempting a landing.

Eileen was putting up a gallant performance, and whenever he suggested a rest she shook her head and tugged away at her clumsy oar; there was more than a suspicion of zig-zag to their course, but at least they were still moving forward roughly in a safe direction, and now drawing nearer in, edging across the current. It was going to be a hard slog, and they could see some areas of broken water to their left.

Suddenly Eileen stopped rowing, and it was not from exhaustion. She pointed.

'Look,' she said wearily, 'we're back where we started – that's our island, I know it, I'm sure it is ... don't you see? That's where we climbed the rocks – oh James, it's too much, after all this...'

'I believe you're right,' he said, and he knew she was.

That broken water over there was where the reefs began, somewhere over there they had sunk the cruiser with the body of her husband, only that morning, in the sunlight. Now they were back. It had all been for nothing. He let the boat drift.

There was no point in tearing their guts out any more. He just sat and stared out over the dark unfriendly water to the even more unfriendly darkness of the island. There was no justice. It was just a damn great joke, on them.

Eileen had lowered her head down on to her oar. Beaten. Dear God, what could happen next? Presently she lifted her head.

'That stuff in the sack there,' she said.

'Those were some of the things we were running short of, at the bungalow, especially the bread and milk. They must have left some men behind when they took us away–'

'They were scared that a search party might arrive,' said Hellier. 'I'm sure that's why they left the island.'

'So they took us there and back again, and we didn't even guess.' She began to laugh softly, and it ended in a sob. 'Right back here where we started – all for nothing…'

'Let me have that oar,' he said. 'You've had enough, you go and sit – we can't spend the night out here in this little boat … we'll have to land somewhere.'

'Couldn't we just go on rowing?' she pleaded. 'At least we're on our own, away from them – we might get picked up, there must be other ships around here, there must–'

'It's miles for any regular route,' he said. 'We both know that … that was why your husband chose the island.'

'Fortune Island!' Her voice was bitter. 'A return trip to nowhere at all – and don't tell me to cheer up because I don't think I could bear it.'

'The oar,' he said gently. 'Take a little rest – we're still at liberty–'

'I'm sorry,' she said. 'I must be getting hysterical … just don't mind anything I say for a bit.'

'Sanest woman I ever met,' he said. 'I'll row a while and we can plan the future.'

'You still think there is one?' She let him take her oar and she clambered aft.

'The weather's in our favour,' he pointed out. 'If there had been any wind blowing we couldn't have got this far. We have acquired a small supply of food, and we have several hours of darkness in front of us – if only we knew for sure which way we ought to be pointing we might push on and see how long we could last... I'm no navigator, though, and it wouldn't be any picnic once the sun got at us ... oh hell, look at that!'

Behind them two bright bursts of light flickered in the sky and slowly floated to the water, lighting up the sea and spluttering on the surface for a few seconds.

'Signal flares,' said Hellier. 'They must be desperately anxious to locate us to take a risk like that – they obviously don't want anybody to know they're here, and those flares could be seen miles away. If they had squirted them off earlier they would have got us ... they must know now that we didn't land anywhere near that point, so they'll be making a circuit of the island ... look, here comes that blasted ship!'

The *Blue Virgin* was showing more light now, and the course she was on would take her between them and the open sea.

Hellier reckoned she was about half a mile

away, and now he was pulling steadily to the shore, there was no alternative. They would never reach the open sea in time, the next flare would show them up. Dodging inshore was the only thing they might hope to do, and the *Blue Virgin* would have to keep well clear of the reefs in the dark.

They could hear the engines over the water; seabirds, resenting this intrusion, squawked and wheeled in the dark sky, and James Hellier was rowing like mad and hoping that Eileen was watching out for the coral reefs because he hadn't time to turn and look, and their boat had no rudder.

Another flare rocketed into the sky, but it must have been partly a dud because there was little illumination this time, and all of it was out over the sea on the open side.

'Three rousing bloody cheers,' Hellier panted.

The next flare was no dud; it rose ominously high, broke into brilliant light and seemed to be taking an unpleasantly long time to sink, so that for minutes on end the surrounding sea was as bright as day. The only good thing was that the flare was floating on the seaward side of the *Blue Virgin* – they were making sure that the rowing boat had not slipped beyond into the open sea.

Hellier was giving his rowing all he had left, an outcrop of rock suddenly appeared with no warning, and he splinted an oar, which slowed them up and made their final progress crab-like and tortuous, and he could hear himself snorting with his inelegant technique.

Eileen was kneeling up, her face anxious and tight.

'Nearly there,' she called. 'Steady–'

They hit the beach with a bump that dislodged Hellier and he lost both oars, and the stern of the boat slewed round in the shallow water. Eileen stepped in waist-deep, and she had the sack, and she didn't need him to help her ashore. There was nothing they could do then about the boat, they had to leave it there, they couldn't pull it higher up because the beach shelved too steeply and there were too many rocks in the way.

The *Blue Virgin* wasn't moving, which might mean they had been seen – more than likely, Hellier thought. All he had in mind was to get them under cover somewhere.

They had come ashore some two or three hundred yards north of where he and Eileen had done their swimming. The higher ground was to their left, and they couldn't have picked a spot further from the bungalow – for what comfort that might be. He was wondering just how many men had been left behind on the island, there might be a posse out after them already. He had Captain Esposito's gun tucked in his belt.

One gun, and he was quite the world's worst shot. So. He took the sack from Eileen and helped her up through the rocks, and they had absolutely no time for any conversation.

And that was just as well because he had no clear idea of what they might hope to do next, if anything.

They kept to the edge of the high ground, where the jungle thinned and where progress in the dark wasn't too murderous as long as they were ultra cautious, a yard at a time; they could still catch occasional glimpses of the sea, and the *Blue Virgin* made no appearance – if she was making a circuit of the island she was being very fussy, or else their abandoned boat had been found.

After some hazardous slithering about, much of it on hands and knees, Hellier thought he had hit on a good spot. It was dry and sheltered, with rocks overhanging so that in the dark there wasn't too much risk of a search party stumbling over them. When daylight came it would be a different matter, and they would cope with that when it happened. A slice of clear starlit sky was visible, but they saw no more flares, whatever that might mean.

'I have a theory,' said Hellier. 'I fancy Ramon and the gang don't like much being around here in daylight, perhaps because they don't like the idea of somebody arriving in search of you and your husband – and somebody will be arriving here very soon, tomorrow. They know that. So all we have to do is remain undiscovered until rescue arrives. Simple.'

Eileen was squatting under the overhang of the rock, her shoulder against his. 'I've stopped hoping,' she said. 'Anything you say … if I close my eyes I could sleep for a month.'

'Rations for the troops first,' he said. 'That's what all the military books say to raise morale, should be a cooked meal, but we can't run to that, besides, the milk won't keep.'

They had bread and cheese and a bottle of milk each, and after a while she slept, his arm around her. He could have done with a cigarette, but it would be far too risky, and they had no cigarettes left now. So he kept his vigil. He hoped he was right, about Ramon being nervous of daylight on the island, only sunrise would show that, and that was still hours away.

One thing was painfully clear: if Ramon rounded then up again they could expect nothing from him. Nothing but the worst. Looking down at Eileen's pale sleeping face, he felt the slow surge of anger beginning inside him, and involuntarily he tightened his arm so that she stirred and her eyes opened.

'It's all right,' he said softly. 'It's all right.'

Chapter Thirteen

He had to wake her before dawn. He whispered, bending so that his lips touched her ear: 'Eileen, Eileen ... quiet – somebody coming... Eileen...'

She came awake slowly, uncertain. 'Listen,' he whispered. There were sounds from the high ground behind them, voices, men thrashing through the bush, the snapping of branches; nothing stealthy. They heard a deep chesty laugh, and a cheerful obscenity, followed by a cackling burst of enjoyment, and more colourful profanity.

A sharper and more distant voice said: 'You quit that fooling, you hear? You all git yourselves moving–'

A clear young voice, frighteningly near, so near that it seemed to come from just over their heads, said: 'Ain't nobody heah–'

'You git moving like I said, Sashie boy, and you button your lip – you hear me?'

'Sure thing.' Sashie didn't sound too enthusiastic.

They heard the chink of his boots over the rocks, behind them. Hellier was kneeling, one hand on Eileen's shoulder to keep her still. The other members of the party appeared to be moving off, not too quietly. Discipline wasn't too good.

In a mutinous undertone Sashie said something about a lot of goddam foolishness, then he was coming down, and Hellier pressed Eileen further back under the overhang of the rock, his fingers hard on her shoulder. He was watching that small open space in front, and hoping that Sashie would go on further down to the beach below.

He didn't. He slithered the last few feet on the top of the rock and landed right there in front of them, but with his back to them, no more than five feet distant; they could hear his breathing, and Hellier found himself unable to swallow.

Sashie looked very young and slight, long in the leg wearing tight slacks and with a gun, a rifle in his left hand. If he turned he would surely see them. Very gently Hellier had eased his gun from his waist-band, moving himself into a crouch. A shot now would end it, they'd have the whole lot down there after them.

Sashie yawned noisily; clearly he was no commando. He put his rifle down on the ground, and squatted, and he was so close that Hellier could see the faint shine on his face. Now was the time to get him and Hellier was about to move when Sashie shifted his position. He had a cigarette in his mouth. A match scraped and it made plenty of noise, lighting up Sashie's face. He turned to toss the match behind him, and he saw them and his mouth opened and the cigarette dropped.

Hellier was on him before he could make a move, pinning him to the ground, face sideways, the barrel of the gun rammed hard into Sashie's ear.

'See this?' whispered Hellier.

Sashie saw, his mouth opened and then snapped shut, his eyes as well. He was very still, except for a slight quiver.

'Make a sound and I'll blow your head off – you got that?'

Sashie's lips shook. He looked about sixteen, a pretty boy with long lashes and a full mouth and a smooth unshaven skin. Very pretty. And very scared. Hellier was kneeling on his arms, quite ungently and using all of his weight, so that Sashie whimpered in spite of his manifest willingness to co-operate, and he did not enjoy the gun in his ear. Now he began to weep quietly.

'Quiet you,' said Hellier. He pushed Sashie's rifle over so that Eileen could take it, then he twisted one fist into Sashie's abundant and heavily oiled dark hair and began to drag him back further under the overhang, and Sashie offered no kind of protest.

'He's only a boy,' said Eileen, making

room for them.

'He can talk,' said Hellier. He slammed Sashie over onto his back and settled himself on Sashie's chest, the gun less than three inches from Sashie's mouth. The whimpering stopped.

'Please, boss, you no shoot – I be quiet … you don't shoot, please!'

'That's up to you, boy,' said Hellier. 'You give me half a chance and I'll ruin your looks for good.'

Sashie rolled his eyes desperately towards Eileen. 'Lady, you no let him do this!'

'Not so loud, boy. Keep it quiet.' Hellier slowly waved the gun backwards and forwards in front of Sashie's face.

'If anybody else comes it won't help you. You get it first. Understand?'

'Sure, sure, boss, you the boss!' Sashie's white teeth gleamed.

'Good,' said Hellier. 'Now we'll all be quiet and listen.'

Sashie's stomach heaved, lifting Hellier up and down. And Sashie's breathing was noisy. But there was no other sound. From time to time the prisoner papped his lips and swallowed, in a state of acute misery. There were faint voices shouting in the distance, but no real sound of any alarm at Sashie's absence. The search party was moving on, and Sashie was showing not the slightest desire to do anything, but what he was told. He was too young and raw for this kind of thing on his own.

Presently Hellier shifted his weight and squatted so that Sashie's breathing became less of an effort, but he kept the gun in view.

'All right,' said Hellier, 'maybe you'll live a little longer.'

'You no shoot?'

'Not yet,' said Hellier. 'You can stop crying. Just don't upset me, that's all – how old are you?'

'I am fully a soldier,' said Sashie. 'I am old enough to fight. I am sixteen and two months, so I am now a man, yes?'

'You can sit up,' said Hellier, 'but don't do anything heroic, you're too young to die. How many men were in your party?'

Sashie sat up, carefully. 'Our orders were to look for you and the lady, there were six of us–'

'And you were the lucky one,' said Hellier, 'but it won't get you any medals this time. There were just the six of you, that's all?'

Sashie was happy to oblige with all he knew, why not? This man kneeling beside him with that gun, he was not like anybody Sashie had ever had dealings with before.

'There were the others,' said Sashie, 'from the ship, they are looking on the other side, and we are to meet them–'

'How many?'

'I do not know that, boss, I did not meet

181

them. Perhaps ten from the ship, perhaps more – the Señor Ramon is a most angry man, I think.'

'It wouldn't surprise me,' said Hellier.

'Most angry man,' said Sashie. His shirt was too big, and in their brief encounter it had been torn. Nervously he was trying to tuck the collar in, and he was doing his best in that confined space not to look Hellier in the face.

'I'm not very happy myself,' said Hellier, 'which is why you're here, boy – am I right?'

Sashie nodded. He was remembering all the things he had heard about this man, and they did little to comfort him in his solitary position. This was not how Señor Ramon had been telling them it would happen. There was no glory to be won here.

With nothing but his own bare hands this man had almost killed Didi, and Didi was a famous fighter with a knife who feared nobody. Sashie sobbed quietly to himself at the thought. He was a good boy, he drank little, and he had not yet been with a woman as a man should be, properly. He had many things to live for, and he did not want to die here under a rock alone in the darkness.

Señor Ramon had promised them many things, but not this. It was not just. The Señor had said a man could face death with honour and in the company of his fellows, for the liberty of their people. The Señor made grand words. But he was not the one with a gun in his face – and that man watching him.

Sashie rocked backwards and forwards, his hands clasped over his stomach, remembering the prayers of his not-so-distant childhood, the prayers which Señor Ramon always said were so foolish.

'What are you going to do with him?' Eileen had the rifle awkwardly across her lap, unwilling to have anything to do with it.

'Squeeze information out of him,' said Hellier. 'All he knows.'

Sashie shivered and edged closer to Eileen for protection. Eileen moved the rifle to the other side of her and put it on the ground so that Sashie couldn't reach it. He might be just desperate enough to try anything. Hellier nodded at her and lifted a warning finger.

'Hear that?' he whispered. Engines ... must be the *Blue Virgin* coming round the coast...'

Clear on the night air they all heard the even beat of engines, very steady. No flares. They saw the ship slowly pass across the open view they had of that small slice of sea, the beam of a torch jittering now and then. The *Blue Virgin* was close inshore, Hellier guessed about two hundred yards out, no more, but there were no coral reefs on this side.

Sashie was sweating copiously.

Hellier patted his shoulder. 'Good boy,' he said. 'Now let's have some facts, we've got the rest of the night to pass, so we'll have all you think you know, right? First of all, who is Ramon and what is he after here? Make it quick.'

Sashie's look of surprise was so instant that it had to be genuine. 'But surely all the world has heard of Señor Ramon Luba?'

'Sorry,' said Hellier. 'Not me. What's his particular claim to fame?'

'He is a famous man,' said Sashie, puzzled. 'It is a fact.'

Hellier smiled at him and shook his head. 'Famous for what?'

'Ramon Luba?' said Eileen. 'I've heard the name, I think I've read about him somewhere ... he's been in the news for something or other.'

Sashie was looking a little less piqued at this partial vindication. 'He is our great leader,' he said.

'I've guessed that much,' said Hellier, still smiling. 'Where is he going to lead you?'

Sashie took a deep breath, he knew this part. 'Señor Ramon Luba will restore our liberty, he has fought long for us, now his hour has come, and we will share in the glorious victory.'

'That's fine,' said Hellier.

A small flicker of courage came back to

Sashie. 'You make it a joke, it is no joke–'

'Too true,' said Hellier. 'It's going to mean sudden death for some of you – when is all this going to happen, and what has it got to do with this island?'

'It is a secret,' said Sashie, with some dignity. 'You are not one of us–'

'You still anxious to be a dead hero, boy?'

'James,' Eileen murmured, 'you wouldn't kill him–'

'I would.'

'James – think … you couldn't do it!'

'If I have to choose between him and us I'll strangle him – there won't be a sound… Sashie, my boyo, you might start praying.' Hellier rubbed his hands together, flexing his fingers.

Sashie swallowed, licked his lips. There was nowhere he could look but right at this man. Hellier tilted Sashie's chin with the fingers of one hand, and Sashie went stiff.

'We go to Mercanda,' he said. 'That is our mission of freedom–'

Hellier sat back on his heels, he laughed softly. 'You must all be crazy, so you're going to liberate Mercanda? Is that what Ramon has been telling you? Mercanda?'

'It is all planned,' said Sashie. 'It cannot fail–'

'You're quoting Ramon once more,' said Hellier. 'He must have you all mesmerized … how many men have you got?'

'We are to form the spearhead,' said Sashie stolidly. 'When they see us the people will rise with us–'

'And you believe all that?'

'It is planned,' said Sashie.

'It's pathetic,' said Hellier. 'You haven't a hope in hell of pulling it off, not even if you had a real army–'

'We will have the support of the people–'

'My son,' said Hellier, 'That's been the epitaph of more busted revolutions than you've ever heard of – when I was in Mercanda two days ago there were so many armed guards you couldn't spit without getting into a court-martial – they're ready for you, believe me.'

'We plan to surprise them, the people of Mercanda have been under the hell of the tyrants too long, they will welcome us, you do not understand these matters.'

Hellier glanced at Eileen and shrugged. 'Cannon fodder, it's enough to make you weep.'

'I go now? Please – I have told you...' Sashie shifted about. 'I will not tell them where you are, I promise... I will say nothing of this–'

'So I suppose you've been using this island as an arms dump, is that it?' said Hellier. 'This is the nearest place to Mercanda – just a short hop across the water. How long have you been using the island?'

'Two times before this I have been here, at night, there was nobody here, at first—'

'Then the owner of the island turned up, and that made it different, you found you couldn't come and go as you liked, so the owner had to be removed – up the revolution and to hell with anybody else!'

Stiffly Hellier rose to his feet, and Sashie continued to eye him with much apprehension; his hopes of an early release from this frightening position were fast fading.

'Amateurs!' said Hellier disgustedly. 'A bunch of bungling amateurs, led by a criminal lunatic … you'll all get yourselves slaughtered, you realize that?'

'The people will rise with us,' said Sashie dutifully.

'Like hell they will,' said Hellier. 'They're doing quite nicely over there as far as I saw, better than most of the islands around here – I saw no signs of any civil unrest anywhere.'

'We have been working in secret, our plans are well made. Señor Ramon has been in the revolution for many years—'

'And he's still looking for a job,' said Hellier. 'Listen to me,' he went on with sudden harshness, 'did Ramon tell you they've just bought a frigate over there? Not a new one, but a frigate all the same – you know what a frigate is?'

Sashie lifted one shoulder and thought. 'A

187

little battleship–'

'It'll be big enough for the job it has to do,' said Hellier.

'It will not be stopping us,' said Sashie. 'Our plan will be to land there by night.'

'I'm not really getting through to you, am I?' said Hellier patiently. 'Haven't you ever heard about radar and searchlights? Why do you suppose they acquired a frigate just at this time? There's been a leak, they know something about your lot, they must do, they're over there waiting for you, and as soon as you show up they'll blow the *Blue Virgin* out of the water, and your comic little revolution will go phut!'

A look of growing uncertainty was creeping over Sashie's young face; he wiped his hand over his mouth.

'It is not possible,' he said, but without too much conviction. 'Señor Ramon knows what he is doing–'

There was a burst of shouting in the distance. Somebody calling: '*Sashie-e-e-e!*'

'If you try to answer them it'll be the last sound you ever make,' said Hellier.

'They will come back,' said Sashie.

'You'd better hope they don't.'

'If you let me go,' said Sashie, 'I will not tell them you are here.'

The calling continued: '*Sashie-e-e-e … Sashie-e-e boye-e-e!*'

'They'll think you got the wind up and

nipped off back to base,' said Hellier. 'You're too young for this.'

'I can shoot a gun,' said Sashie. 'I am enough of a man to do that, and I am not afraid.'

Hellier smiled. 'You're doing all right, but you're still too young. Ramon must be having a recruiting problem if he takes them as young as you – where's the money coming from?'

'Señor Ramon,' said Sashie, 'he arranges that, when we have removed the government there will be plenty of money–'

'Loot, but I'm afraid you won't see any of it. When is the invasion?'

'Tomorrow night, at midnight we land.' The answer popped out promptly, and Sashie realized too late what he had said.

'Lucky for you we grabbed you' said Hellier. 'You won't have to join the suicide squad – doesn't that make you feel better?'

'They will come and look for me until they find me,' said Sashie. 'They will not leave me.'

'Leave it to me,' said Hellier. 'I'll find somewhere nice and snug.'

'You will kill me? You mean you will kill me?'

'Mightn't have much choice. You or us.'

'James,' said Eileen quietly.

Suddenly Sashie made a loud retching noise and clapped a hand over his mouth, rolling his eyes and hunching his shoulders. He retched again very distressingly.

'Feel sick,' he mumbled. 'Very bad sick...'

'If you're going to spew you do it over that side,' said Hellier hastily, shifting out of the line of fire. 'Don't mess the place up.'

One hand still over his mouth, Sashie crawled out, got shakily to his feet as though looking for a convenient spot. He staggered a few steps, then began to run blindly forward, flinging his arms wide.

'Hey, you!' snapped Hellier scrambling up.

There was a wild high-pitched cry, and Sashie disappeared from view. The cry went on and then died abruptly below. Hellier got as far as the sharp edge where the rocks broke, and he had to lie on his belly to look down.

It was nearly sheer for some fifty feet, then a dark spread of rocks and then the sea. He could just make out the body sprawled there below, and he could detect no movement or hear no sound, just the sea.

'Did he mean to do that?' Eileen lay beside him. 'Is he dead?'

'I think so ... but I'll make sure – I don't think he knew what he was doing, he was only a kid–'

She touched his arm. 'Would you have killed him?'

He looked at her briefly, then away again.

'You stay here,' he said.

'James, if he isn't dead…? You won't just leave him there?'

'His mob had your husband killed, and Ahen Toong, they're planning to stir up merry hell in Mercanda, you heard, didn't you? All right, if he's alive I'll do what I can … that satisfy you?'

'He was just a kid, you said so yourself–'

'Man enough to use a gun, on you or me if he had to.'

She lay there and watched him begin the climb down in the darkness. That scene with Sashie might almost have been play-acting, except for that unearthly cry Sashie had let out as he was falling, and her own stomach was turning over at the memory.

Hellier seemed to be down there a long time, and she was unable to see just what he was doing. But he didn't call up to her or try to make any sign and she knew what that must mean. Sashie's comrades were no longer calling for him.

When Hellier rejoined her his breathing was heavy, and he lay for a moment with his head pillowed in his hands.

'He broke his neck,' he said. 'He couldn't have felt a thing… I covered him with sea-weed, they won't find him, not too soon–'

There was a silence between them while he lay and caught his breath. 'There was nothing I could do,' he said.

'I know,' she said. 'But he – he was so frightened.'

'He had every right to be, he was one of them, only a kid, I know – but he was putting us both in danger. Don't blame me, blame Señor Ramon Blasted Luba.'

Wearily he pushed himself upright. 'I'm sorry about Sashie, but I am glad I didn't have to decide. He chose his own way, maybe he didn't know what he was doing, I don't know... I don't want to think about it. Now we'd better crawl back into our hutch and see what comes next. If we can last out tomorrow we ought to get through – at least we have some information to work with.'

He turned her so that she faced him. 'I'm not a monster. We couldn't have let him go, you know that.'

'I know,' she said.

'He shouldn't have got himself mixed up in this nonsense. He believed everything he was told – Ramon the Saviour! It's enough to turn your stomach.'

'What can we do?' she said.

'We wait,' he said. 'Tomorrow's coming.'

Chapter Fourteen

Once more they heard the beat of the *Blue Virgin's* engines going slowly past; the sound was alarmingly close and sharp, and Hellier fancied he could feel the vibration shaking the ground where they lay, and he covered Eileen's hand with his to keep her still although he knew nothing could be noticed of any of their movements – a much stronger light had been rigged up on the ship and they could see its reflected glare over the water and the cliffs in front of them. The *Blue Virgin* took a long time passing, and he thought he could hear voices.

The search was being intensified. They'd be using every man they could raise, and this time the job wouldn't be so haphazard.

'I think I can hear them,' he whispered. 'Lots more of them, more than before ... they're doing it properly now, not all that shouting. I don't think we can stay here... Sashie found us, they might if they really organize themselves. They'll be looking for him as well, and they know he was somewhere in this area, so we ought to shift ... listen, when I was down there, down the bottom by the water, I saw a place, sort of a

cleft in the rocks, we could squeeze into it
… and there's plenty of seaweed to cover the
front … you take the sack and I'll take the
gun, Sashie's gun – think you can make it?
It's steep but it's all right … it's better than
here…'

She just nodded, and collected the rem-
nants of their supper into the sack. She
didn't want to go down there near Sashie's
body, but there was nothing else to do. She
wanted to lay her weary body down and
weep herself to sleep.

'Hurry,' he whispered.

As she crawled after him to the edge of the
rocks the sound of men's voices was very
near, and she didn't dare look behind. No
matter how carefully she moved the bottles
in the sack chinked, and the sack itself got in
her way. The sea murmured darkly below. It
was years since she had done any climbing,
and it had never been like this. She couldn't
see where they were going, but she felt his
steadying hands on her legs. Placing each
foot right for her, whispering encourage-
ment.

She was to do just what he told her and
they wouldn't hurry. She understood. And
she wasn't to look down. She understood
that as well – she couldn't look down there.
There were moments when all her muscles
refused to obey, when they all locked on her
and lost their power, and she remained

flattened against the rock, while his calm soothing voice told her she was doing fine and not to worry.

He coaxed her into movement again, gentling her until she stopped freezing and whispering that she couldn't do it – because she knew she had to. He took the sack from her and dropped it out of sight and it made little noise, falling on the dark heap of the seaweed. Foot by foot they came down. Her legs ached and trembled, and there was a sharp pain between her shoulder blades from the pulling on her arms.

When they came to the loose scree and her foot slipped and dangled in space he held her hard, pining her against the rock with his weight, and then inching her back to a safe foothold.

'Good girl,' he whispered. 'Nearly there – not long…'

When the sound of the shot came it stiffened them both, and they would have fallen if they hadn't reached an angled point where their weight was jointly poised inwards. Just one shot, above them on the high ground, very close. A man shouted angrily and was answered just as angrily, but there was no more shooting. Just one random shot from a trigger-happy searcher, perhaps. Her mouth was dry with dust where she had her face pressed up against the rock. She wanted to cough and clear her throat, dust trickled down by her neck and along her stretched forearms. A few more minutes of this would be more than she could bear.

The voices above them went on. The name Sashie was being repeated, several times, but now they weren't calling out for him, just talking about him ... wondering what happened to him?

The warning pressure of Hellier's arm in the small of her back kept her motionless. Now she was sure they would be discovered, just as soon as one of those men came over to the edge of the rocks and looked down, the natural thing to do beside the sea. She didn't think she could hold out any longer, and it wasn't only the strain on her arms and legs.

Hellier had worked himself up so that they were almost on a level on their perch, and she could see his face close to hers, and he was smiling, really smiling, as though they were taking part in some elaborate game on those cliffs.

'All right,' he whispered. 'They'll move on...'

Her throat tickled intolerably and she swallowed gritty dust and clenched her teeth, closing her eyes ... and she had a vision of them falling together down to the rocks where Sashie lay under the dark mass of the seaweed.

There appeared to be some kind of a discussion going on above, slow and deliberate; when somebody laughed hoarsely nobody else joined in. It wasn't possible to hear what was being said, and the rise in the rocks above made it difficult to see if a torch was being used.

Hellier was trying to think if they had left any trace of their presence up there, if they had forgotten to bring anything in their hurry to climb down. He was feeling the strain of holding her steady, he had to make a slight adjustment of his weight, a loose piece of rock slipped away under his foot and he could do nothing as it began to roll down, gathering impetus and other pieces of rubble. The noise sounded enormous to them, shattering ... but it had been a small piece of rock and there was the unceasing sound of the sea to cover everything. Eileen whispered something that might have been a prayer or a sob. Nobody came to look, and Hellier realized how unmercifully he had been holding her on the face of the rock. The voices were moving off, and from the spasmodic shuddering of Eileen's back he guessed she was weeping with relief, and he felt better himself.

He waited for a while until he knew she was still, and for the first time he was aware of the breeze on their backs in from the sea. 'That was close enough,' he whispered. 'All right now?'

She was clinging to the face of the sloping rock. 'I'm frightened to move,' she said, 'I know I'll fall…'

'You won't fall,' he told her. 'Don't move until you feel ready, loads of time now. Just relax – you're not going to fall – don't even think about it … now we're going to move down sideways, to your left, bit by bit … plenty of places for your feet…'

He was guiding her diagonally across the area of scree to firmer rocks, less steeply angled, and now she was following his lead. There was no disaster.

He skirted the dark mattress of weed that hid the body of young Sashie. He showed her the split rock with the triangular opening.

'Room for both of us inside,' he said. 'It's dry. It smells a bit, but it'll be safer than up aloft.'

He unslung the rifle and got down on his hands and knees and crawled in through the opening; he struck one of the matches he had taken from Sashie's pocket. There was very little space inside, and the air smelt rank and fishy; it wasn't so much a cave as a natural fissure in the rock; there was very little headroom and the further end sloped sharply upwards; there was some sand and he saw no crabs – or anything else that might scare her. He struck another match as she wriggled in behind him and sat against the rock.

'Not exactly commodious,' he said. 'But it'll do.'

She shuddered. It was like a tomb. And the smell...

'We won't be spending long inside,' he said. 'Just when it looks dangerous. I'll drag up some seaweed so we can hide the opening if we have to ... they'll never find us here, not unless we give ourselves away.'

They crawled out into the air; he went back and picked up the sack from where it had fallen on the piled seaweed, and he was glad to note that the empty milk bottles were unbroken. He thought he had heard the sound of trickling water while they had been making their descent, and water was likely to be more than important in the course of the day that lay ahead.

He located the trickle, in between some of the smaller rocks, a tiny apology for a stream, but water all the same. He let it flow quietly over his hand and tried it. Brackish and not too cool, but fresh water. They had bread and cheese, and now water. They should survive.

He got both bottles almost filled and started back down, and he had to exercise extra caution not to lose his precious load. He was regretting now that he hadn't taken the cigarettes that had been in Sashie's pocket with the matches; but then Eileen would surely have guessed where they came from because she knew they had none left of their own. He was hoping she wouldn't realize that Sashie's body lay under the seaweed just a few yards from where they were proposing to make their hideout.

If there had been more time he would have piled some rocks on top of the seaweed; it would be hell if some seashore scavengers dug up the body.

When he told Eileen what he was going to do she raised the objections he expected – mainly that she didn't want to be left there alone. He went on undressing, down to his pants.

'I'll be quicker on my own,' he said.

She watched him go carefully down to the water and wade in; when he swam it was very quietly and soon he was out of her sight; she knew she could never have kept up with him.

He swam just a few yards out from the shore, using a breast-stroke that made no ripples and no noise; he was taking a chance on what currents there might be around the island, so he wasn't going to be too far out at any one point, and he wasn't going to lose sight of the shore. Further, there was the small matter of sharks – they were, he hoped, unlikely to be so close in.

He rounded the north point with no trouble and in flat water; it was different then, the waves slapping at his face and slowing him up, pulling him out where he didn't want to go; there were those coral reefs out there, and he wanted no part of them. But he chuntered on, keeping the trees on the skyline and the high ground. He saw no torch lights, no sign of any movement, and he spent some time treading water and watching, trying to get his bearings.

Moving closer in he fetched up against some sunken coral and scraped his toes, but was able to float on into clearer water – if he had been swimming with his normal vigour he would have been very sorry. Gently did it.

He thought he must be very near the place where they had left the rowing boat; there were the rocks clustered right down to the water.

But he couldn't see the boat – which was the sole object of the excursion. There had been just a slim hope that the boat hadn't been found. Perhaps he hadn't got the right place. He pulled himself out of the water. All the rocks looked the same. It might have been further along. They hadn't waited to secure the boat, so it might have floated off.

He straightened up to look seawards. The shot from the high ground behind him split the air and splinters flew from the rock right there beside him. They had been up there waiting for him. The second shot wasn't so close.

He plunged in, ducked under and swam as fast as he could, straight out, until his ears were singing. He surfaced slowly, gulped some air and went down again. They would expect him to go back the way he had come, so he was aiming straight out, the further out the better – unless they had rigged up a good light they would never follow his progress, he hoped.

He was heading out to where the reefs were, but he couldn't do much about that, not yet. He couldn't keep up the submerged stuff too long, so he turned on his back and floated. He could see the island now, and a light flashing on the place where the shots had come from – and the rowing boat coming up now between him and the shore; it had a light and he could pick up the flashing of the oars, two rowers pulling – perhaps the very boat he had been hoping to take. But not yet heading his way.

He remained still on the water, and he heard the shouting between the boat and the men on shore; the light was searching the shore, close in, moving along, almost parallel to the route he had taken ... they had probably had him under observation from the time he came round from the top. That first shot should have got him.

The rowing boat had gone ahead of him.

Keeping his eyes on it he began to swim gently along; it was about eighty yards away, he reckoned … four men, two rowing, one with the torch up for'ard and the other steering.

After a while they appeared to have stopped, then the boat went about and back for a few hundred yards, and he let himself sink until only his nose was getting any air, trying not to disturb the surface, and he was taking on more sea water than he needed. They couldn't possibly pick him out, not in that light, unless he did something foolish. He could hear them talking now and then when he grabbed some air they were that much nearer. If they came on they would have to see him.

He saw the boat turn broadside on and continue its passage north, the man in the bows was standing up now, flickering his torch over the waves, and the rowing was faster.

Hellier let the rest of his body float up and relaxed. After that he needed a rest. His legs were beginning to feel heavy and he had been forced to swallow more sea than was good for him. He swam quietly along and saw the boat rounding the northern point and go slowly out of his sight, the light flashing about in front of it. So they had guessed that he had come that way.

If they caught Eileen unawares – the whole

business would have been for nothing. She would surely hear their oars, and get inside the hole in the rock. She wouldn't panic.

He quickened his pace, there was now no need for caution, and he had the current to contend with. Until now he had been feeling full of energy and resilience, and it was only when his stroke became clumsy and his breathing ragged that he knew he was tiring. That dark bulk of the island seemed to stay put, it didn't appear to come any nearer.

If he failed now, if he found he couldn't make it after all … he allowed himself a breather, still paddling on his back, his eyes closed. Twenty even strokes, then another twenty…

He turned over and tried his slow long-distance crawl, concentrating on the rhythm, checking his route every thirty strokes, no snatching, no hurrying, feeling the strong pulling on his thighs and shoulders. The smoothness was coming back.

If that damned rowing boat turned back he'd swim slap into it. He made the point, a little further out than he had hoped, but he hadn't lost his bearings in the dark – the one thing he had really feared. He saw no boat no light flashing on sea or shore. Just the dark cliffs and the high ground with the jungle, and it was then the most beautiful sight he could recall. He was pointing the right way, all he had to do was go on swimming and get there.

There was no kidding himself, he was rapidly tiring; no matter how he varied his stroke he was moving much more erratically. If he didn't get a jerk on they could row that boat right round the island and catch him on the second lap – an ignominious conclusion.

He used up everything he had left; his pants had drifted down below his hips, weighted with the water, so he kicked them off. He got there, just. He sprawled on a rock and coughed up brine and grunted, and he didn't want to move – the relief was wonderful.

He pushed himself upright, got to his feet like a weary old man. When the beam of light caught him it was as sudden and as unexpected as a slap in the face. He just couldn't have been more defenceless.

A flat voice said: 'I have your clothes. Come very carefully – there are three of us and we would be happy to shoot you.'

Gingerly he began to pick his way over the rock, the blinding light following his every movement. It was not the most heroic moment in his life. One of the men laughed, and said: 'You enjoy your little swim, yes?'

'Very invigorating,' he said. 'What have you done with her?'

A bundle of clothes hit him in the face, his slacks and shirt, and he could now see the three of them, with carbines – and the hole in the rock where Eileen should have been.

The beam of the torch played over his body. The witty one moved forward and jabbed him in the groin with his carbine before he could cover himself: 'Git the clothes on, man, you don't look so goddam dangerous to me – you ain't gonna be bothering with no little lady this night.'

He started dressing, and when they thought he wasn't fast enough they gave him the treatment, clubbing him in the ribs, and also in more sensitive areas as the fancy took them. Three to one. The right odds.

Chapter Fifteen

Eileen was the first person he noticed when they at last got him back at the bungalow. There were some twenty or thirty men around the veranda, smoking and talking and just lounging like troops off duty; nobody appeared to be in charge of them, and they crowded round when the prisoner arrived, offering cheerfully obscene advice as to what should be done to him.

Eileen sat by herself, looking angry. Ramon was there in the sitting-room, and Esmée in uniform, but not Captain Esposito; there were no guards. The storm blinds had been drawn and the room was stifling.

When Hellier came in and blinked in the light, Ramon nodded. 'What a fool,' he said.

Eileen stood up. 'I'm sorry,' she said. 'I heard the boat and I thought it was you – and then it was too late–'

'I hope they didn't rough you up,' said Hellier.

'I'm all right.'

He smiled at her. 'We were out of luck.'

'I shouldn't have let them find me,' she said. 'But I was so sure it was you–'

'What a touching reunion,' said Esmée. 'You could have saved yourselves the trouble.'

'A stupid performance,' said Ramon. 'I took you for a man with more sense – what good has all this done you?'

'You'd be surprised,' said Hellier. He found himself a chair; two of the men who had brought him in remained just inside the door to the veranda.

'Well now,' said Ramon. 'We are here again.'

'Took the very words out of my mouth,' said Hellier. 'We've done this before – how is the gallant Captain?'

Ramon nodded at the two guards by the door and they withdrew; there was some laughing outside.

'Sashie,' said Ramon quietly. 'Tell me about Sashie.'

Hellier glanced at Eileen. 'Have you got any idea what he is on about?'

She shrugged. 'He seems to have lost somebody called Sashie, I can't make head or tail of it.'

'So sorry, Generalissimo,' said Hellier.

'They are playing the fool with you,' said Esmée.

'Very easy to get lost out there in the dark,' said Hellier. 'It took you some hours to find us, if we'd had a little luck you would still be looking. Perhaps he deserted.'

Esmée got up from her seat and stalked over to stand in front of him, legs apart, one hand on the unbuttoned holster of her revolver. Her face was streaked with sweat and her tiny teeth showed.

'You are sounding very satisfied with yourself,' she said. 'I wonder why?'

'I laugh that I may not weep,' said Hellier. 'Why all this fuss about one absentee? You've got lots of suckers out there, with guns and things—'

Quickly she raised her hand and swung at his face, and there was nothing feminine in her movement. He caught her wrist in mid-air and held it without moving from his seat.

'You slap me and I'll slap you right back,' he said, 'even if Uncle Ramon is watching. I'm no gentlemen in these circumstances.'

'Esmée,' said Ramon, 'we have men to do that much better.'

She took a deep breath, and it was not to demonstrate the conspicuous modelling of her breasts. 'I will have you flogged,' she said in a vicious whisper.

'You'd enjoy that,' said Hellier.

'Not yet, Esmée,' said Ramon.

Hellier swung her wrist backwards and forwards – the love-hate bond between them. He could have pulled her onto his knee. He smiled and her breath hissed at him.

'Doll baby with a gun,' he said softly. 'We

don't ever get together properly, do we?'

'Swine,' she said, with no venom.

'Well there's always Didi,' he said, 'or did I ruin him for good?'

There was another burst of laughter from out on the veranda – perhaps they had seen through the mesh screen on the door. Hellier let Esmée's wrist go. She was looking confused and angry but she didn't go for her gun, and somehow he had guessed she wouldn't.

She glared at Ramon. 'He is playing with us–'

'Mrs Dempster,' said Ramon with quaint formality, 'you will stay where you are–'

Eileen had got up and was walking to the door. She turned. 'This is my property,' she said. 'I didn't invite you here and I don't wish for your company. I am going to take a bath and change my clothes, and I will not have any of your armed thugs following me about my own house.'

She sounded quite magnificent, and she positively swept out of the room before Ramon could think of what might fit the situation. Presently they heard the taps running in the bathroom. Hellier stretched and his ribs reminded him that he was not altogether in top condition.

'I could do with a drink,' he said. 'I don't think our hostess will object. Anybody join me?'

Esmée's face was sullen with suspicion and uneasiness. 'He is different,' she said. 'He knows something.'

'Hellier,' said Ramon, 'I have been more than patient with you–'

Hellier put a finger alongside his nose. 'First things first, remember, you are an uninvited visitor here. I need a whisky.'

'Take him out and shoot him,' said Esmée.

'Then you will never know what I know,' said Hellier. 'I see you have been helping yourselves.' The whisky and some glasses were on the side table near the door into the dining room. He poured himself a drink and two pairs of eyes watched him as though he had been performing a clever trick. 'Up the revolution,' he said and drank.

He carried the rest of his drink back and took a seat right opposite Ramon, and Ramon's eyes had become bright and sharp beyond his years, and Esmée had drawn closer to her uncle.

'You should have put him into the sea when I told you,' she said.

'I do wish you'd get your mind off that particular aspect of the situation,' said Hellier. 'It distresses me, especially coming from a pretty girl like you.'

'You still do not think we are serious, I will show you how serious we are.' With a creditable flourish she drew her revolver and levelled it at him and her hand was quite steady. 'Now,' she said, 'talk to us now.'

'You've still got the safety catch on,' he said. 'However, the good word is Mercanda – how does that suit you?'

She turned to her uncle, lowering the gun automatically. And Hellier reached forward and took the gun out of her hand and put it in his lap.

'Not that I'll be needing it,' he said. 'I just think it'll be safer with me. I dislike fire-arms, and I know you have all these armed men outside, so don't misunderstand me–'

'Señor Hellier,' said Ramon, 'you must realize that you have now put yourself in an impossible position, you and the lady. We must get rid of you both, there is now no other way left to us.'

Deftly Hellier rearranged the gun so that now it was pointing vaguely in Esmée's direction. He put the safety catch off.

'I'm a lousy shot,' he said, 'but I ought to get one of you, I don't mind which, so I wouldn't call in the troops if I were you.'

'You cannot carry this through,' said Ramon. Esmée muttered something vicious under her breath, fingered the useless belt about her middle, and darted a look at the door, full of fire and anger. But she didn't move.

'I can keep this up for a long time,' said Hellier.

Ramon shook his head sadly. 'Foolish.'

'Mercanda is the magic word,' said Hellier. 'I'm saving you all from sudden death, most of all those dopes outside – you'd need a modern army with full equipment to pull this off, and you haven't an army, it will be a massacre–'

Ramon waved a hand to shut him up. 'My name is still remembered,' he said, 'and we have many friends in the right places.'

'Oil,' said Hellier, 'that's the attraction, isn't it? Mercanda is going to be rich so you want to make sure you get your slice – you didn't read the signs right, you're too late… I'll make a bet with you – by this time tomorrow you'll either be dead or in jail, all of you. You've picked the wrong time and you haven't the organization.'

'Mercanda is ours,' said Ramon. 'My family gave it good government for many years, and I will find all the allies I need when the time comes. I have not been wasting my time in exile, Señor Hellier, I have worked for this, and when the people hear that I have returned to set them free–'

'You sound like the father and mother of God,' said Hellier. 'Doesn't your conscience bother you at all?'

'I will do what I know in my heart has to be done. There is no fear in me.'

'Paranoia,' said Hellier.

'I am sane,' said Ramon with a quaint touch of dignity. 'You cannot insult me, you are nothing–'

The voices of the men outside had become louder and more excited. The door was flung open before Hellier could issue any further warning about what he might do with the gun in his hand, and the young man who rushed in without any weapon took no notice of the tableau he was interrupting. He looked at Ramon, panting.

'Señor, there is a ship coming – a ship with lights!'

Ramon got up and stalked to the door. Hellier looked at Esmée and shrugged and put the gun down. He stood up.

'After you,' he said.

There was pandemonium outside, men milling about and shouting and pointing, streaming down off the veranda. Ramon was pushing his way through them, waving his arms and shouting to restore order – they were to put out their cigarettes – all of them were to get under cover – he would have silence! It took several minutes before he had them under some kind of control, scattering to hide under the bushes very reluctantly, all of them wanting to watch the ship out there on the water. It became almost quiet.

Hellier had followed Esmée down off the veranda to where they would get a better view of the sea, and together they watched the searchlight moving over the water, about a mile out, flickering on and off, and the moving lights of the ship.

'The navy from Mercanda,' he said softly. 'Item, one second-hand frigate heading this way, I think ... but I don't see the *Blue Virgin*.'

'She has gone.' Esmée's voice was abrupt. 'We are not that stupid ... they will see nothing here.'

'Interesting,' said Hellier. 'It means they know about you.'

'They will not come ashore.'

He looked at her. 'Whistling in the dark. They know all about you, that's why they're here ... you've had it.'

She shook her head, but said nothing. Then Ramon joined them, walking stiffly and silently over the grass.

'You should not be here,' he said sharply. 'You will keep out of sight, you understand?'

'I promise I won't wave my hankie at them,' said Hellier. 'They know you're here, there's nothing you can do ... unless you're crazy enough to think you can fight, then they'll blast the place to hell – is that what you want?'

The bright beam of light was fingering the rocks and the cliffs, swinging slowly about and about, then just as slowly it began to shift upwards, white and dazzling.

Ramon tugged Hellier down beside him on the grass, and Esmée flung herself down.

Ramon shouted and waved at his men, motioning them down. The light bathed them through the twisted branches of the trees, moved left and then right, and climbed on up above them, working grotesque shadows in among the tree trunks, blanching the stiff tufts of grass.

Hellier found himself watching Esmée's face so near to him. She was frightened, moistening her lips and shielding her eyes.

'Phut goes a revolution,' he murmured. 'It was doomed from the start – timing is everything, and you and Uncle Ramon chose the wrong time.'

'It is not over,' she said.

The wide cone of light had moved on, higher up, and Hellier realized that it would miss the bungalow at that angle, the trees would hide the buildings unless the ship came back on her first course. Some ten minutes had passed since the light had begun its probing, and the men hidden under their bushes had got over their first scare and were murmuring among themselves ... if only one of then would strike a match and light a cigarette, there would be night glasses trained on the island ... something to hold their attention was needed.

When he started to get to his feet Esmée grabbed at him and pulled him down.

'You stay with us,' she said savagely. 'It is not over!' There was a wiry strength in her

216

slim body and her eyes were fierce at him.

'Relax,' he said, grinning. 'I can wait.'

She released her grip on his thighs. 'I am remembering,' she said, 'for later–'

'There isn't going to be any later,' he said. 'You might as well face the sad facts – you and Uncle Ramon here should have pushed off on the *Blue Virgin* when you had the chance–'

Ramon had got carefully upright. 'They are moving on,' he said very quietly. 'They have found nothing, they are going.'

Hellier stood up. 'Damn,' he whispered, 'oh damn and hell to it...!'

Ramon chuckled, actually chuckled. 'You are a man with no luck,' he said gently. 'Not so?'

Now the frigate was clearly not heading in, and she was further out than Hellier had guessed. She was broadside on long enough for him to know for sure that she was the frigate, which only made it worse. She was keeping well outside the broken line of the reefs, still moving, still swinging that light, but now the wrong way.

Ramon was holding his arm in a nervous trembling grip. 'You see,' he said triumphantly.

'I see,' said Hellier. 'Hullo and goodbye.'

'It was a routine night cruise,' said Ramon, 'and they have seen nothing here, nothing! That is good, no?'

'No,' said Hellier.

Groups of men were coming out of hiding, laughing, relieved.

'Now you will give me back the gun,' said Esmée. 'You will be having no use for it … and you say you are a bad shot.'

Her sharp little teeth gleamed at him in the dark as he handed over the gun, and suddenly he could smell the heat of her lithe body as though a tap had been turned on.

Her wide wet mouth glistened. 'You have been amusing yourself with us too long, we are a big joke to you … now that is over, finished, there is nothing for you to hope for…' She tilted her head to one side as though seeing him for the first time, inspecting him all over again.

Then she gave a high-pitched giggle. 'I have never made love with a dying man – it might be good…'

'If that's a last minute offer,' he said, 'you'll have to get your kicks elsewhere.'

She was shifting against him, her face mocking and her hips beginning to move on him, as unsubtle as a whore's bargaining. In her free hand she held the gun, safety catch off, the other hand reaching for his neck.

Ramon had missed the interlude, he was looking with special intentness back through the trees. 'What is happening there?' he shouted and began to run.

Through the branches there was a sudden

flicker of flame, small at first and then quickly bursting into bright yellow and crimson, leaping high and rolling smoke.

'It is the house!' said Esmée. 'The house is burning–'

Before she had taken a couple of strides Hellier had passed her, then Ramon, and now he could smell the smoke and he could hear the roar of the flames leaping. He was the first to reach the grass in front of the veranda, and by then the front of the bungalow was all blazing and the windows were cracking and the heat belched so that he had to shield his face long before he got to the veranda steps – and he saw no sign of Eileen. And he knew also that it would be suicide to try to get in that way, the roof was about to go and the floors would be nothing but blazing timber.

Some of the others were coming up. He scrambled round the end of the veranda at the rear where he desperately hoped the fire hadn't yet reached. But it had, it was even fiercer than in the front, and the sound of the flames was terrifying … the agony of not being able to do anything made him sweat in spite of the scorching heat … in a matter of minutes the bungalow was being reduced to nothing but a shell.

He was crouching by the back door into the kitchen, he had pulled his shirt up over his head to cover his mouth – it would be madness but he had to do it, he had to force his way in there somehow.

There was a strange shrill cry behind him, almost a scream– *'James ... James...'* Outside and behind him – and he saw her by the concrete building where the pump worked and she was beckoning to him frantically. He stumbled over to her just as a mob of excited men began to appear round the corner and Eileen tugged him back and they both began to run, ducking behind the outbuildings, away from the glare. If anybody had noticed them leaving nobody seemed ready to take up the pursuit yet, the fire offering much more exciting possibilities.

'Do be quick!' Eileen panted. 'I hope it won't go out too soon...'

'Not much chance of that,' he said. 'Thank God you weren't caught inside – I wonder how it started?'

'I did,' she said. 'I couldn't think what else to do... I saw that ship going off and I couldn't bear it, James – so I got some of the fuel from the pump room and sloshed it all about and lit it and ran...'

They were pushing into the edge of the jungle. There was plenty of shouting behind them, but nobody chasing after them. Ramon's voice was shrill and full of force, screaming instructions at his men.

'They'll never put that lot out,' said Hellier. 'Listen to it roar!'

'James,' said Eileen, pausing in her stride, 'you weren't thinking of going inside there, were you? You were, weren't you? I could have wept when I saw you by the door–'

'I don't know what I was thinking,' he said. 'I thought you might be inside.'

She grabbed him by the shoulders and kissed him roughly. Her face was smudged and her hair smelt of smoke and charred timber.

'James,' she said...

'You saved me from a fate worse than death,' he said. 'Esmée had me cornered with a gun in my ribs. I was as good as dead, she said – and she had some kinky notion of making me bed down with her on the grass – don't laugh, the crazy wench meant it ... that's a hell of a good blaze you started.'

They could see the flames leaping high above the tops of the surrounding trees, and the smoke was drifting high and spreading. It was like the eruption of a miniature volcano in the darkness, and it must be visible for miles around.

'They can't miss that on the frigate,' said Hellier. 'I just don't believe they can all be that sloppy ... they'll have to come ashore and look, they obviously suspect this place...'

They found a spot that gave them a view of the sea; the frigate was coming about in dramatic fashion and at speed, the searchlight fingering the shore as it swept by.

'This is where we keep out of the way for a bit,' said Hellier. 'There's likely to be some confused shooting, and the less we have to do with it the better.'

Chapter Sixteen

He was aiming vaguely for somewhere on the north side of the island, as far as possible from the probable scene of conflict, and he had to tow Eileen after him regardless of how she was feeling, and she admitted she wasn't feeling too good. Every minute might be important, there would be no joy in getting themselves shot up by both sides in the dark – the men from the frigate might have old fashioned ideas about shooting first and saying sorry afterwards.

It was all of fifteen minutes before they heard the opening shots, mostly ragged rifle fire down by the shore, answered after a pause by heavier automatic firing that sounded better controlled. The bungalow was blazing away, evidently deserted now.

'This is no place for us,' said Hellier. 'We're strictly spectators – how are you managing?'

'Hilarious,' she said. 'Do we have to go much further?'

'Elsewhere and fast,' he said. 'Let them shoot each other to hell and gone, they don't need us.'

The firing went on sporadically for nearly half an hour, and it was impossible to guess how the battle might be going, but they were still shooting, and that was enough for James Hellier. Now and then they caught a reflected dazzle from the searchlight, and the air was full of strange jungle noises. A very unquiet night, and dawn nearly over the horizon.

Eventually there was a sharper and heavier thump, and they ducked as they heard the shell whistle overhead, high up, screaming, and they didn't hear it land.

'That's the real hardware,' said Hellier. 'A sighting shot – I hope that clot Ramon will have enough sense to throw in his hand–'

Rifles were still banging away. When the frigate's gun barked again there was a splitting explosion high up on the hill behind where they lay, and they felt the ground jump and heard the trees crack, and branches sailed through the air for seconds after.

Eileen was shaking, deep dry sobs that she was probably not aware of, and there was nothing he could do but hold her tight and keep her down. If those gunners decided to pepper the hillside, to do their job systematically – Hellier had an unhappy picture of a slender steel muzzle poking out of the turret and looking for them ... wham-bang and that would be it.

Huddled together they waited and waited. The next shell was a long time arriving, and he became illogically angry because they had to wait. There was a scattering of small-arms fire, but it didn't sound important now. Even men shouting somewhere in the distance – shouting or screaming, it was impossible to tell which. He wondered how many men they had landed from the frigate ... it sounded like an untidy mopping-up operation.

When the third shell came it landed almost as soon as they heard the gun – there by the bungalow. Blazing wreckage was tossed high in the air. A direct hit as near as mattered. So those gunners could shoot. Too close for comfort – and now the trees were burning all around the area down below them, and the smoke was drifting up to them, and they had to shift again, this time in a really smart fashion.

'If we stay here we'll fry or choke,' said Hellier. 'And if we try to get down there some trigger-happy ape will pick us off ... this isn't our war. They're still shooting at each other, we'll let them get on with it.'

'Neutral,' said Eileen and smeared her streaked face with a dirty forearm. 'Suits me.'

'It'll be dawn soon,' he said. 'So let's move.'

They moved on; they had to get clear of that blinding choking smoke that billowed up to them; there was as yet no way of telling how the fire might spread and overtake them, but it seemed to be moving dangerously fast in their direction, breaking out in all kinds of unsuspected places; the noise itself was beginning to be more frightening even than the shooting had been ... and still they could hear an occasional shot far off.

The frigate didn't open up again; it had done its job with economy – the target was alight and there would be no place for Ramon and his men to retreat to or hide in – or for James Hellier and Mrs Eileen Dempster, unless they were lucky.

From the position they were in they couldn't see anything of the frigate's search-light, and Hellier was trying to work across to the swamp he remembered – the damper the better this time. They saw the flames reach up the hill now behind them, there were blood-chilling animal sounds high above the crackling of the burning jungle, birds wheeling crazily through the smoke, the spurting hiss of vegetation in the heat, and the enveloping stench of scorched greenery and jungle growth. It would be suicide to let themselves be trapped in the bush – there were the rocks and the cliffs, and the sea ... they mustn't let themselves be cut off from the sea, it was their only chance.

If there had been any real wind they would

never have made it from where they were, Hellier knew that. Even as it was, there were some ugly spurts of flame licking across their route as they dodged out into the open near the coast and saw open sky and the pink and faint yellow where the sun was about to show.

They slithered down among the damp rocks and the sea smell was wonderful after what they had been smelling back up there. They could look back and see what they had missed, and what had missed them by such a narrow margin.

'I'm afraid your property has taken a beating,' Hellier said. 'Scorched earth all over...'

Eileen knelt on the damp sand and ran both hands over the brittle ends of her singed hair. 'I won't want to see any of it again,' she said. 'Ever.'

He felt in his pockets and he knew very well he had no cigarettes. Or anything to drink, which was far more important, after all that scorching smoke and heat

'There's the sun,' he said. 'Looks kind of bogus, too beautiful from here.'

It was more than beautiful, and it arrived very quickly, right on cue; magnificent and serene; a couple of pelicans wobbled awkwardly on the foreshore, looking comically severe; they could see the smoke thinning behind them, and birds still squawked their irritation at being evicted from their trees.

'We'll give it plenty of time to settle,' said Hellier.

'And then?' Eileen was rinsing her face in the sea very gingerly with cupped hands.

'We'll introduce ourselves to the captain of that frigate,' he said, 'and cadge a ride back to civilisation, no trouble – you can probably sue the Mercanda government for war damage. In the meantime I'll join you in the cloakroom, I might even paddle.'

'James,' she said slowly, 'what are you going to do – I mean afterwards when we get away?'

He joined her by the water's edge, scooped up some water and washed some of the grime off his face. 'I'm not worried,' he said. 'Look for a job, I suppose – that's what I came here for in the first place, seems a long time ago. I might even take a trip back home to England, I've still got a ticket.'

'I see,' she said. She was going to say more, she had turned to him.

'Damn,' he said softly, 'look at that out there.'

It was the frigate, heading out to the open sea, at speed. Hellier stood up and waved his arms frantically in the shallows, capering up and down, shouting idiotically as though they could hear him. He shook both fists and the frigate continued on course.

'The stupid lot of bastards!' he said with feeling.

Eileen moved a little higher up the beach and sat down, her face bleak.

'Well,' she said wearily, 'so we're still here – I don't think we'll ever get away...' She began to weep quietly to herself, her face in her hands. Why not? Hellier could have wept himself.

Smouldering grey ash and stripped and stunted trees marked the wide path of the fire; there were thin wisps still trickling up into the nice bright sunshine. There was little left of the bungalow – the blackened shell of the walls and twisted metalwork, and a ragged hole where the grass had been in front of the veranda; debris all around.

The first body lay sprawling on the ground near the path, and he was too slow to stop Eileen seeing it as well. They found six more, all of them lying on their backs and with the grotesque boneless attitudes of sudden death. There would be more scattered about in the bush. He saw none of them wearing any kind of a naval uniform, just the khaki slacks and shirts.

He had to hold Eileen while she was being sick, but she would go on with him, and now there was nowhere to leave her on that disaster of an island. There were more bodies lower down the path, and one he recognized, lying in front of the others. Señor Ramon had at least died at the head of his troops.

There was no sign of Esmée, and for some odd reason he was glad of that. The jetty was undamaged, and they made their way down to it and sat by the water; the air was cleaner and it was as far as they could get away from the rest of the island.

Eileen had become very quiet, her face pale and her eyes blank; not wanting him to touch her or speak to her. Soon they would be needing water, and other things, and he was wondering if he could salvage anything from the wreck of the bungalow. The frigate had cleared off, evidently after a complete victory, and it might be some time before anybody from Mercanda came over to inspect the battlefield.

In the meantime Eileen sat like a zombie, her shoulders hunched. He was hungry and thirsty and very dirty, and very short of sleep. Nothing to smoke.

Later in the morning a silver twin-engined aircraft appeared and did some low circuits. Hellier waved at it. He thought they had been seen, because the aircraft made a low run across the bay and then went off in the direction of Mercanda.

'Shall we move out of the sun?' he suggested, eventually.

'No thank you,' she said. 'I don't want to go up there again. I'm going to stay here.'

There was no point in arguing with her.

He wandered back along the boards of the jetty, and the sun on his back reminded him that water should be his first objective. There wouldn't be any food left in the ruins of the bungalow, and they might have to spend more time on the island, perhaps another day and night, and he found the prospect less than entrancing.

He avoided the path because he didn't think he could stomach another view of the bodies there, in the hot sun. He scrambled around and got up by the bungalow, and started to poke about in the debris; the roof had gone and he was ankle-deep in ash wherever he moved. He had to heave charred timbers out of the way before he could get at the remains of the kitchen.

After considerable effort and much cussing, he located the deep-freeze, buried under a heap of rubble; the heat had warped the door, and it opened when he gave it an angry tug. A lot of the stuff inside had been ruined, but the tinned goods seemed reasonably intact, and he made what he hoped would be a fair selection. There were bottles of lime juice and orange juice, but they would need water. The Coca-Cola might be the answer, so he added half a dozen bottles; it wasn't his favourite drink, but it would have to do.

He unearthed a sack in one of the concrete outhouses behind the pumping plant;

he couldn't find any crockery, but he felt justifiably satisfied with his labours; they would manage, and it couldn't be for long. Surely somebody from Mercanda would come to survey the battlefields.

So humping his sack he started back, and when he came in sight of the jetty he was happy to see that Eileen had moved – more than that, she was waving to him and pointing out to sea, and long before he reached her he could hear the delighted note in her voice and see the change in her face – it was suddenly radiant once more.

He saw the reason for it all in the large white motor cruiser sweeping into the bay in dramatic style, a very smart job – with a man squatting on the forepeak and waving at them in the friendliest fashion.

Eileen grabbed Hellier's arm. 'Look! Look! That's Tom Davidson's boat – isn't it wonderful, isn't it?'

'Good,' said Hellier, dumping his sack. 'But is he on our side?'

She shook his arm excitedly laughing. 'He works for my husband...'

'Then it's about time he showed up,' said Hellier.

The cruiser slid up to the jetty and before they had made fast Tom Davidson was ashore. He was a tall shambling man with a little paunch and a balding head. He bounced forward, his hand outstretched and the widest of smiles on his face.

'My God, Mrs Dempster, are we glad to see you! I wouldn't have known you – what's been happening here?'

'Everything,' said Eileen. 'This is Mr Hellier–'

'Howdy,' said Davidson. 'Excuse me, but you do look pretty rough – are you okay, Mrs Dempster? We heard all kinds of crazy rumours back on Mercanda – they even brought in a load of prisoners, said they came from here, first thing this morning – been some kind of a battle here, they said ... you mean it was true?'

Eileen nodded.

'Good God,' said Davidson. 'So old Ramon finally got around to it.'

'You know about him?' said Hellier.

Davidson laughed. 'He's been a bit of a local joke for years, always threatening to invade Mercanda ... I didn't think anybody took him seriously.'

'They did last night,' said Hellier.

'So we've been hearing. A battle, no less – it sounds crazy.' Davidson wiped his bald patch. 'You sure you're okay, Mrs Dempster?'

'Yes,' she said flatly. 'It was a battle all right. We were here.'

'You'll find the casualties up there on the slope by the path,' said Hellier, 'if you're interested. Ramon as well.'

'Best thing that could happen to him,' said Davidson. 'He could never have lived through another jail sentence. He had a record as long as your arm, but he always came back for more. Crazy. They got the girl, Esmée – did you come across her?'

'We did,' said Hellier. 'What will they do to her?'

'She'll probably serve a spell in jail, then they'll most likely ship her out somewhere – how's Mr Dempster? Is he with you? We heard he didn't arrive at St Lucia, and we've been kind of worried–'

'My husband is dead.'

Davidson looked at Eileen and then at Hellier, and Hellier just nodded.

'Dead?' said Davidson. 'Good God – how?'

'I think I'd like to go aboard now.' Eileen's voice was stiff and she was looking at nobody on that crowded jetty in the sunshine.

'Sure, sure,' said Davidson, not quite certain what to do next.

It was Hellier who helped Eileen aboard in silence. 'Thank you,' she said and went below into the cabin. She closed the door.

'Eddie Dempster dead? I can't believe it–' Davidson was about to follow Eileen.

'Leave her,' said Hellier.

Davidson examined him in a noticeably unfriendly fashion. 'I heard your name, it didn't mean anything to me, Hellier–'

One of the crew had picked up the sack Hellier had dropped on the jetty. 'You want this?' he called out.

'Not any more,' said Hellier.

'What happened to Eddie Dempster?' Davidson wasn't going to move.

'He was murdered,' said Hellier, 'before I got here.' Wearily he gestured towards the sunlit island. 'It looks like a pleasant spot, it's nothing but a mortuary, take it from me. If I could have a drink and a cigarette–'

'Anything for us to collect, up there?' said Davidson.

'Not a thing, the house is in ruins, burnt out last night ... go and see for yourself, you won't find Dempster's body, it's under the sea, plenty of spare bodies, but not Dempster's – satisfied? There's nothing up there you need now.'

Davidson shrugged and squinted up at the island, still unsure what he ought to do next. 'He was a good man to work for, Eddie Dempster.'

'I never had the chance to find out,' said Hellier. 'I came here to meet him about a job. I didn't see him, but Mrs Dempster was here ... he was dead then but she didn't know it – ever since then we've been on the run from Ramon ... was he quite crazy?'

'Maybe,' said Davidson. 'The Luba family used to be big people in Mercanda in the old days, but that was all over long ago, the trouble with Ramon was that he couldn't believe it, he still thought he could come back – a hell of a nuisance.'

'I can think of another word,' said Hellier. 'He talked of a rising in Mercanda–'

'Not a hope,' said Davidson. 'That was his dream. Ten or fifteen years ago it might have worked, not now, there's too much stacked against him – he could never see it. One or two cranks might have shouted for him, if he won ... he hadn't a hope. We saw those flares here last night, so they sent the frigate to investigate, they've been expecting trouble–'

'He was using the island as a jumping-off ground,' said Hellier. 'Storing arms. It was all right until the owner arrived and took up residence. That fouled up the Ramon strategy – he'd been expecting to have the island to himself. So Dempster was eliminated, along with his servant, and I found the bodies soon after I got here – that was the start ... if you could organize me something to drink I'll give you a blow-by-blow account of the rest – it's not a very pleasant story.'

Davidson nodded. 'How's Mrs Dempster been taking it?'

'I don't think I've ever met a woman like her,' said Hellier. 'She was pretty amazing all through.'

'I hear they hadn't been getting on too

well,' said Davidson thoughtfully. 'All the same, it must have been a hell of an experience for her–'

'It was,' said Hellier. 'I didn't enjoy it much myself.'

They brought him an ice-cold beer; the first pull on a cigarette made him giddy and reminded how long it was since he had eaten.

'I know of a Caribbean island going dirt cheap,' he said. 'The present owner doesn't favour it much.'

'That figures,' said Davidson. 'Too many corpses.' Then, briskly to the listening members of his crew: 'let's go now.'

A little later, when Fortune Island had already dwindled into a dark blob on a shimmering horizon, James Hellier tapped on the door of the cabin; he had a tray and some coffee.

She let him in, and she had tidied herself in some miraculous feminine fashion. She smiled at the tray and he realized once again what a very attractive woman she could be.

'I seem to remember that you've done this before,' she said.

'Old Faithful,' he said. 'Always at your service.'

She patted the bunk beside her. 'There are so many things I want to say to you ... please.'

He poured her coffee, held it out to her

and then sat beside her. 'Plenty of time now,' he said. 'Just drink that.'

She smiled and held out her free hand. He took it in both of his and said: 'You look fine.'

'Thank you, James Hellier,' she said softly.

The publishers hope that this book has given you enjoyable reading. Large Print Books are especially designed to be as easy to see and hold as possible. If you wish a complete list of our books please ask at your local library or write directly to:

Dales Large Print Books
Magna House, Long Preston,
Skipton, North Yorkshire.
BD23 4ND